ALL OR NOTHING

A NOVEL BY

BLAKE KARRINGTON

Copyright © 2007 by Blake Karrignton
Published by Dynasty Publishing
5585 Central Avenue
Charlotte, NC 28212

www.dynastybooks.com

This is a work of fiction. It is not meant to depict, portray or represent any particular real persons. All the characters, incidents and dialogues are the products of the author's imagination and are not to be constructed as real. Any resemblance to actual events or person living or dead is purely coincidental.

Editor: Tiffany Davis

Cover Design: Marion Designs
                www.mariondesigns.com

Book Layout: Lisa Gibson-Wilson
                Renaissance Management Services
                www.renmanserv.com

First printing January 2007

Printed in the United States of America

ISBN 13:   978-0-9752589-5-8
ISBN 10:   0-9752589-5-8

DEDICATION

This book dedicated to:

My Mother, Viola Nash
My Daughter, Kayhla,
and
My Nephew Patrick
(Keep your head up, and you will be home soon)

CHAPTER 1

"Damn! Pass the blunt, nigga." Shantell suggested. "I want to get high, too."

Shantell Bryant, the local stripper, sat in the passenger seat of the car. Currently she was on her way home from a long night at the strip club. Business at the club had been a little slow that night. In an effort to take her mind off everything, Shantell called the weed man so that she could buy some marijuana.

At least if she got high, the night wouldn't be a total waste. Of course, she had no real intention of purchasing any weed from him. She would work something out with him, just like she always had. It was nothing for Shantell to swap sexual acts for drugs or anything else she wanted. She saw nothing wrong with it, to her it was "fair exchange no robberies."

Paul, the weed man, currently had that bomb-ass weed in the hood. He made money hand over fist from the Purple Haze that he sold; it seemed like everybody and their mother was smoking.

It also seemed like Paul got all the pussy. Since he made house calls at all times of night, all kinds of opportunities came his way. One would be surprised to know who he was sleeping with. It wasn't just strippers, but also classy professional women with nine-to-five jobs. Paul had a variety of pussy to pick from.

Shantell grew irritated at having to wait for the blunt. "Damn can I smoke?" She fussed at Paul. "We already did you. Can I do me now?"

Shantell was tight. She didn't like waiting on anyone or anything. Dudes usually waited on her, not vice versa. Now, with her body slightly turned in anticipation of receiving the blunt, she was a little pissed off by Paul's selfishness. From the sweet aroma of the blunt she could tell that it was some quality shit; this wasn't any of that home-grown nonsense. One would have to be a real smoker to know good weed from bad weed, just by the scent. Shantell had a nose for it. It was sort of an acquired skill that came with lots of usage.

"My bad, Shawty!" Paul said. Before he passed her the blunt, Paul inhaled deeply one last time, then blew out a gigantic cloud of smoke. This further annoyed her. Shantell fanned the smoke with her hand to keep it from irritating her eyes. She didn't want smoke in her eyes, but rather in her lungs.

"I'm sorry bout dat shawty. Here you go. Take that to the head; that's all you. You deserved that after that bomb ass head you gave me. Shawty, you da truth. fa real!"

As Paul spoke, all Shantell could see was his mouth full of gold teeth. He had shiny, gold fronts on all of his teeth, which had suddenly become the rage in the South. His skin complexion was jet black and he had a head full of baby dreadlocks, which he proudly sported. He was a down-South nigger for real. Paul represented the Dirty in everything, from his choice of clothes to his car.

Paul shook his head slowly at the mere memory of the blow job Shantell had performed. There was no doubt in his mind that she was a beast when it came to that. It was always a pleasure doing business with her.

Being a stripper had its advantages for Shantell. She knew all the movers and shakers of the underworld. At one time or another they came through the strip club in search of a good time. In life, most times it's not what you know, but who you know. Associations, often could take a person far in the streets, just like in the cooperate world.

"Nigger, don't talk me to death." She replied. "Just pass da fuckin' blunt." Shantell snatched the blunt from his hands almost before the words left her mouth. She fell back into his custom–made, butter-soft, red-and-white leather seats and took a long pull on the blunt. She held her breath for so long that she began to feel light–headed; then, and only then, did she exhale. From there on out, her breaths became shorter and her tokes on the blunt became longer.

Shantell was an avid weed smoker. It seemed like her day didn't go right unless she had something to smoke. She used the drug to take her mind off her miserable circumstances. Meanwhile, Paul smoothly maneuvered his cherry-red, 1986 Chevy Impala through the streets of Charlotte, North Carolina. It was nothing for him to drive while he was high because he had built up such a high tolerance for weed. He drove all the time and never worried about getting pulled over by the police. It took more than one blunt to impair his driving skills.

He drove with great care. His car was raised by hydraulics, so it sat ridiculously high in the air. Its windows were so darkly tinted that it was virtually impossible to see inside. The wheels were 24-inch TOYO tires, with sparkling chrome deep-dish rims. The vehicle was Paul's pride and joy.

"Paul, where you get this shit from?" Shantell asked. "This that shit, right here."

"Shawty, you know I can't tell you that! Then what would you need me for?" Paul announced. "Those that know don't tell; those that tell don't know."

"Whatever, nigger!" Shantell thought to herself.

The recent influx of Mexicans to the populace of Charlotte had bought not only an increase of people, but also an increase in illegal drugs; marijuana and heroin the two most notable. Now, good quality drugs weren't as hard to find. No longer did drug dealers from Charlotte have to depend on out-of-towners for potent product. Paul was one of a select few drug dealers who had tapped into that Mexican drug pipeline.

"Shawty, wanna ride wit me…" Rapper Young Buck of G-unit chanted. "…we can get low."

Paul turned up the volume of his car stereo system. The silence in the car had been killing him. His trunk and back windows rattled violently as the music flowed out of the kicker box and speakers. Both parties involved seemed to be enjoying the music thoroughly. Shantell smoked and bobbed her head to the beat. For the moment, she was carefree.

Shantell was so high that Paul could have put on some rock music and she would have jammed to it. The Chevy's expensive sound system wasn't no joke. To them, it felt like they were in a night club. Shantell was in a zone. The everyday worries that usually dogged her out and depressed her, didn't even cross her mind now.

Despite the lack of customers at the club, Shantell managed to get hers. She had a nice piece of change in her pocketbook, and now she was high off some of the best weed money could buy in Charlotte. She couldn't think of a better combination. What more could she ask for? This was the life for her.

This might have been the "high life" but this wasn't the good life that she desperately sought. Shantell wasn't living. Right now, she just existed. She had stopped living at the tender age of ten; that's when her world began to turn upside down.

As the car crossed the highway overpass, Shantell suddenly came back to her senses. She was now entering her hood, and it was back to the harsh reality that was her life.

As they drove up the hill, on Willis Avenue, Piedmont Courts came into view. Paul glanced over at the dozens upon dozens of ominous–looking, two-story, brick-faced buildings that dotted the landscape. Piedmont Courts was one of the most feared and infamous housing projects in all of Charlotte. It was a breeding ground for lawlessness.

Paul looked over to his left and began to wonder exactly just what he had gotten himself into. *I should have never agreed to drop this bitch off here, He thought to himself. What was I thinking? I musta been higher than a motherfucker, for real!*

"Nigger, could you turn that muthafuckin' music down?" Shantell demanded. "I ain't tryin' to let the whole hood know I'm home. Niggers is nosey out here."

Without saying a word, Paul reached over and turned his music down, giving Shantell the silence she so desperately sought. At this point, he was happy just to get rid of her. Paul didn't like to be told what to do in his ride. What really bothered him was her tone of voice. But he bit his tongue in order to keep the peace.

Rolling down the window, Shantell flicked what was left of the blunt to the ground. She began to brush ashes from her clothes as she prepared to exit the car.

When Paul got to Siegel and 10th Street, he turned and entered the projects. From that point, Shantell's whole attitude seemed to change for the worst. She knew what awaited her inside her home: pain, poverty and despair. Suddenly she wished she didn't have to go home. Shantell would have laid up all night with Paul if she could have. That was, if she didn't have a responsibility to take care of.

If? The word rang in Shantell's mind. *What if?* Her whole life had been a series of questions. In fact, it was one big riddle with no answers. Often Shantell pondered the question, *What if I never was born?*

"Alright, stop right here!" Shantell insisted. "This is good."

Piedmont Courts was well lit. Bright street lights shone everywhere. This cast a dubious glare on the cast of characters who were currently outside at this hour of the morning. There were only two kinds of people out in Piedmont Courts right now: drug dealers and drug users. They were the people who lived their lives outside all governing bodies of the law.

Paul drove his Chevy past all of the illegal activity. Piedmont Courts was one big, open-air drug market. Sights like these weren't new to Paul, since he originally hailed from Fairview Homes, a housing project that was thought to be as equally dangerous as Piedmont court. So it must have been the fact that he was in someone else's hood that left him awestruck and uneasy. Paul didn't come around here much, if at all.

The residents of any housing project were more territorial than a dog. They didn't take too kindly to strangers coming around. It was best just to stay where one belonged, wherever that was. Outsiders, or even the police, had been known to be chased away, by force, from Piedmont Courts.

Shantell's home address was 915 East 10th Street, apartment 16. This was never her home, rather a place where she rested her head. She just lived there. If home was where the heart was, then her heart was elsewhere, far, far away from the ghetto.

Paul hit the brakes and pulled over to the curb. He cautiously scanned the projects for any signs of danger. The drug game was so crazy these days; drug dealers were robbing drug dealers.

He wasn't has worried about Shantell setting him up, but in his line of work, one could never be too sure. One thing Paul had learned from dealing with strippers was that they were basically mercenaries. Their services usually went to the highest bidder. Strippers usually left the club with the guy they felt could give them the most money, whoever they perceived as "that nigger" or a hustler. In Paul's book, there was one thing for sure and two things for certain: money made people do strange things. With that in mind, he wasn't trying to become a statistic of a homicide, or even a robbery, for that matter.

"Yo, Shawty could you hurry up? I'm dirty. I got some shit on me. And the way it's poppin' off out here tonight, the police could be rolling through here at any minute." Paul used the false statement to hide the fear he already had begun to display. He was prepared to say or do whatever to get the hell out of there.

Shantell ignored him. She busied herself taking off her high-heeled shoes. There was no way in hell she was going to get out of Paul's hydraulically-raised Chevy without first removing them. One, she would probably break her neck if she got out the car with them on. Two, her shoes were too expensive to be breaking them or messing them up.

"Bye!" She said before jumping out of his car.

As soon as the door closed, Paul made a U-turn and peeled off. The car made a loud-ass noise and left skid marks in the street. If Shantell was trying to be inconspicuous, she didn't have to worry about it anymore. Paul's hasty retreat attracted lots of attention. His screeching tires woke up half of Piedmont Court.

"Punk-ass nigga!" Shantell cursed as the car raced off. She weaved her way through the obstacle course of crack heads, dope fiends, drug dealers and prostitutes. As she did so, she said a few hellos to some of the resident drug dealers and self-respecting drug addicts that she knew.

From inside numerous project windows, prying eyes fell upon her. Shantell stayed her course, making her way to her back door. The shoes that she clutched in her hand now also served as a weapon, just in case any drug-induced junkie was brave enough to attack her.

Though Shantell was a resident of Piedmont Courts, she was well aware of the fact that her birthplace could also be her last resting place. She had seen it too many times: senseless killings of residents by other Piedmont Court residents. It was rare, if at all, that an outsider came into the projects and killed someone. The residents did a good job of exterminating themselves.

Shantell hated Piedmont Courts with a passion. She couldn't wait till the day came when she could finally get out of there for good. She planned on using everything at her disposal to insure her departure. Right now, that meant using her body, and Shantell was all right with that since she had nothing else of significant worth to use as a bargaining chip. She was determined to get out the hood and stay out for good, by any means necessary.

Finally Shantell reached her door. Quickly she removed her house keys from out of her pocket and unlocked the door. She was greeted by darkness. Shutting the door behind her, Shantell moved through the pitch-black kitchen with ease. Smoking weed had made her extremely thirsty, so Shantell decided to get something to drink while she was still downstairs. She felt for the wall and turned on the lights.

As soon as she did it, Shantell realized her mistake. Literally dozens upon dozens of roaches began to run for cover. The more timid ones disappeared while the bigger, bolder ones continued to feast on the scraps of fried chicken that lay halfway eaten on a plate on the counter.

"Damn this fuckin' house is so nasty!" She swore. "Can't wait to get up outta here." No matter how long she lived in the projects, rats and roaches were two things she would never get used to.

The sight of the roaches repulsed Shantell. However, that was something that could not be controlled. On the other hand, there was no excuse for being nasty, filthy or just plain trifling and to Shantell; her mother was all three, and then some.

After shooing away any nearby roaches, Shantell grabbed from the dish rack a jelly jar that doubled as a drinking glass. She ran the cup under hot water several times. When she was satisfied that it was clean, she reached into the refrigerator and poured herself a glass of tropical punch Kool-Aid. Shantell drunk glass after glass in an effort to quench her thirst. She was so intent upon drinking that she never heard her mother creeping up on her. It was a noise from the floor that alerted Shantell to her mother's presence.

"Shantell!" Brenda Bryant barked. "You finally brought yo' ass home, huh?"

Startled, Shantell dropped the jar, shattering the glass on the floor and sending Kool-Aid everywhere. Her mother almost blew her high with that stunt. Once she came to her senses and realized actually who was behind her, Shantell was pissed.

"I thought I told you to get somebody else to watch ya kid," her mother chastised. "I done raised my kids. I ain't taken' care of no more babies. I'm getting' tired of yo' shit. Nobody told yo' ass to have no baby. Every time I turn around…"

Shantell stared at her mother in disbelief. She continued to stare as her mother ranted and raved. Shantell thought the whole thing was much ado over nothing. It wasn't like her mother had something else better to do; after all, she didn't work, nor did she have any significant other to tend to. No self-respecting man wanted to be bothered with her. Literally, she had no life. Her mother's life had gone up in smoke from the first hit of crack she took. After that, it was a wrap.

Shantell thought her mother should be thankful for even being able to spend time with her granddaughter. Hell, she should be thankful that Shantell even still talked to her. The Lord knew that Brenda didn't even deserve that common courtesy. Not after all that she had done to Shantell.

Instead of looking up to her mother, respecting and loving her, Shantell looked down on her. Brenda Bryant had been on cocaine or heroin, off and on, for most of Shantell's eighteen years on this earth. Shantell always felt like she raised herself. It was a rarity when her mother was in her right state of mind. Drugs had caused Brenda Bryant to neglect her motherly duties. Shantell felt like she never had anyone to give her guidance, or to mold her into a young lady. She blamed her mother for setting her up for a lifetime of failure. What she did learn from her mother was what not to do, instead of what to do. For these reasons, Shantell felt like her mother robbed her of her youth. Brenda was the reason that she was in this messed-up life predicament now, which was why Shantell let her mother make reimbursements in the form of babysitting.

Her mother continued. "You gonna pay me for babysitting. Ain't nuttin' in this world free."

"So this is what this is all about, huh?" Shantell replied. "You want some money, huh?"

Shantell reached in her Gucci bag and pulled out a handful of crumpled-up one dollar bills. She shoved them into her mother's hand. This immediately killed her mother's protest... "Here you go! Take it! You know you want it."

She didn't have to tell her mother twice. Brenda snatched up the money and flew out the door like she was on a mission. She was on her way to the nearest crack house.

"Run along, crack head!" Shantell yelled after her. "Go get high. I hope yo' next fuckin' hit is yo' last, bitch!"

Brenda didn't even bother to say anything in her own defense. She knew what her daughter had said was absolutely true. She was going to take the money and blow it all on drugs, just like she did her monthly welfare check. Just like Brenda did any little bit of money she got her hands on. She had a hell of a drug habit to support and it seemed like it grew worse every day. The mythical monkey that was on her back had turned into a full-grown gorilla.

In this household, mother and daughter were cast in reversed roles. Shantell was the sole provider for the household. It was she who was responsible for the meager furnishings, the food and the rent. Brenda's drug habit had placed her daughter under the gun and kept her there.

Shantell watched her mother leave the house without saying another word. It was a sad day when a child could disrespect their parent like that, without fear of retribution, but this is what their relationship had come to. It was a shame that it had become almost natural for Brenda and Shantell to exchange heated words like this.

After cleaning up her mess, Shantell went upstairs. The first thing she did was to check on her baby daughter, Jordan. Quietly she stuck her head into her bedroom, careful not to disturb her sleeping child. The television provided the only light in the room. It shone on the sleeping baby, as she slept comfortably on the bed. Satisfied everything was okay, Shantell backed out of the bedroom and headed across the hall to the bathroom. She stripped down to her black Victoria's Secret bra-and-panty set. Shantell closely examined herself in the full-length mirror behind the door. With her hands on her hips, Shantell admired herself. She struck a confident pose. There was no question that Shantell was blessed with all the physical gifts to succeed not only in her current occupation, but also in life.

She was drop-dead gorgeous. She stood 5'5 inches tall, with long, shoulder-length hair and walnut brown-colored eyes. Her honey brown skin seemed to radiate. Her waist was small, but Shantell's ass was phat. She could give a lot of video hoes a run for their money. Her body, in general, was in immaculate shape with nice, firm breasts and washboard abs. Shantell's body looked as if she worked out vigorously, yet she hadn't exercised a day in her life. Her curvaceous figure was all natural. If there was such a thing as a body to die for, this was it.

Satisfied with her own physical self inspection, Shantell slipped off the rest of her underwear and stepped into the shower. The warm water pulsated all over her body and Shantell just stood underneath it, eyes closed, enjoying the moment. She wished the water could wash away all the sin from her soul as easily as it did the dirt from her body. Unfortunately for her, it wouldn't be that easy. There was a long road to redemption ahead of her. Shantell had more than a few issues to address before she got right with God or herself. Taking a long shower was relaxing to Shantell. She began to hum her favorite tune by R&B queen Beyonce, as the water gently messaged her body.

"...Me, myself and I that's all I got in the end...I'm be my own best friend." She sang. Shantell sang so beautifully she would have put Beyonce to shame. It was too bad that her talent emerged in the shower. She was too shy to put her talent on public display.

Finally she soaped up twice and rinsed off.

Shantell stepped out of the shower, toweled off, then put her dirty clothes in the hamper. When she left the bathroom she was careful to make sure that she took all her valuables with her. With her mother's drug habit in full swing, if Shantell left any valuables lying around, they would surely come up missing. This was the nature of the beast that she was dealing with. Shantell knew it and understood it well, yet she was powerless to do anything about it, at least for now.

Shantell yawned. Outside her window, she could hear the birds beginning to chirp. To them, their noise signaled the coming of a new day. For her, it was the same old shit, different day.

Shantell climbed into the bed with Jordan. She kissed the infant and whispered 'I love you' into her ear. Shantell looked at her daughter and said a silent prayer that Jordan wouldn't end up like her. Although Shantell's life was far from finished, she didn't like what she was becoming.

After tossing and turning she finally found her spot and got comfortable. Within minutes she dozed off and went to sleep. This was a form of suspended animation that Shantell wished she could stay in. Shantell had more than her share of issues.

To fully understand Shantell Bryant's life, one would have to take a journey into her past.

Chapter 2
The Past: Sugar to Shit

The prestigious, picturesque Ballentyne section of Charlotte, North Carolina represented old money and the white establishment. This tight-knit community was filled with doctors, lawyers, and business professionals. The majority of the city's rich and powerful lived in Ballantyne. There were even a few prominent Black families who also owned homes there, but examples of the Black man's fulfillment of the American dream in the Ballentyne section were few and far between. Most of the minorities that ventured into this area either shopped or worked there. This included Brenda Bryant.

To Brenda, this place was an absolute contrast from her neighborhood. Although only a few miles separated the two, they were a world away.

Brenda was a medium–built, light-skinned woman. One could tell that in her time she must have been an eyeful. Even now, in her mid–thirties, she still exuded some sex appeal.

Six days a week, for the past four years, Brenda boarded two city buses just to make it to work. She was a loyal employee, coming to work even in bad weather. She even came when she was sick, and for good reason: she needed the money.

The Anderson family was the name of the people she worked for. John T. Anderson was a very rich and successful investment banker for Wachovia bank. Charlotte happened to be the second biggest banking system outside of New York City. Brenda worked in the Anderson home as a maid. She carried out all the daily domestic duties like cooking, cleaning, ironing, and even watching the Anderson's twin daughters.

It was Brenda who made their household run smoothly but truth be told, she was overworked and underpaid. Yet she never complained. Brenda loved the Andersons, for whatever reason. Their success in life was like hers, too. She lived vicariously through them even though she knew she would never ascend to that level of life. Still, that never stopped her from dreaming. It never stopped her from wanting a father for her own children. For that alone, she envied Mrs. Anderson.

Usually when Brenda returned home from work, she was extremely exhausted, but not this night. After working her fingers to the bone for the Anderson's earlier that day, Brenda decided to go out on the town. Her friends Wanda, Annie and Sheila kept telling her about a nightclub called Vintage, located on Independence Boulevard. Brenda decided to join them for a few drinks there.

The nightclub was packed, wall-to-wall women and men. During the course of the night, drinks flowed freely. Before the night was over the woman were pissy drunk. They then decided to continue the party at Wanda's apartment, back in Piedmont Courts.

Back then, crack cocaine was ravaging not only the Black community but also the nation. Piedmont Courts was now caught up in the eye of the storm. In these projects almost everybody was on something, even if it was just alcohol.

"Damn, I'm tired as shit," Brenda commented. "I think I'm about to go home."

"Damn, already," Annie said. "Don't be a party pooper! Stay."

"Hang out a li'l longer!" Shelia stated. "We hardly ever see each other anymore."

Brenda was submissive by nature. She was the type who tried to please everybody. As a result, she usually fell short of her own goals that she wanted to accomplish. Often she appeased others at the expense of her own personal happiness.

"Alright, since ya'll put it that way," she replied. "I'll stay, but I can't promise for how long because I'm real sleepy."

The women sat around the kitchen table reminiscing on old times. The liquor continued to flow freely. The woman thoroughly enjoyed each other's company; it had been so long since they all hung out together. Life had pulled them in different directions but, somehow tonight it had brought them back together for a reunion of sorts.

"You still tired?" Wanda asked.

"Yeah. Why?" Brenda asked.

"I got something for you." Wanda insisted. "Wait right here. I'll be back."

Wanda exited the apartment through the back door but before anyone could miss her, she had returned. She clutched something tightly in her fist. Everyone but Brenda knew what it was. Still, the women kept silent.

All eyes were on Wanda. They watched as she went into her kitchen cabinet and removed a clear glass bowl object from the top shelf. Unbeknownst to Brenda, her friends had gotten caught up in the recent drug craze. The project environment had succeeded in stripping them of all their morals and principles. Once upon a time, they wouldn't be caught dead getting high. Not now. Their attitudes had suddenly changed with use of the drugs. To them, getting a little high now and then was acceptable. Every person had a vice; this was theirs.

"Let me take a hit first," Annie begged.

Wanda fired back, "No, bitch! Stop being greedy and show some hospitality. Let Brenda go first."

Wanda carefully placed a small, whitish-looking object atop the crack pipe's stem, then she gently nudged it towards her friend Brenda. Brenda looked at the blackened glass crack pipe in bewilderment. She was unsure of exactly what to say or do. All Brenda knew was that she couldn't disappoint her friends.

Either it was the liquor or the absence of good judgment that led Brenda to take her first hit. Wanda passed her a lighter and she proceeded to set the drug ablaze.

Light crackles could be heard as the heat disintegrated the crack cocaine. Quickly clouds of smoke began to fill the bowl as Brenda began to pull lightly on the stem. In seconds, the drug filled her lungs. In an instant, the drug raced through Brenda's body, clouding her thoughts.

From her first hit of crack cocaine, Brenda was hooked. Never in her life had she ever experienced a sensation like this, not even during sex. Brenda continued to suck on that glass dick all night long. By the time she did go home, she didn't have a dollar to her name.

From that point on, Brenda Bryant was never again the same. Her experiment with drugs would later blow up in her face. She began a slow descent into the murky world of drugs from which she would never fully recover.

❧❧

At first, Brenda was able to control her craving for crack. She simply would lose herself in her work or her two children. Her daughter Shantell and her son Reggie began to play a greater role in her life.

For a time, Brenda even turned to religion to rid herself of those crack demons. At the suggestion of a family member she became a devout Jehovah's Witness. She immersed herself in religion. Becoming a Witness required Brenda to do some field service, which consisted of her canvassing various neighborhoods, going door to door to recruit new members. She also gave away copies of the Witness' weekly publication, *The Watchtower*.

It was early one Saturday morning when Brenda was preparing to go out and do her field service. Looking in the mirror, she inspected her modest articles of clothing: a dark blue wool overcoat, a white blouse and long blue skirt. Satisfied that she met the Kingdom Hall's strict dress code requirements, Brenda grabbed her purse and began to exit her bedroom.

"Mommy, can I go with you?" Shantell begged. "Please!"

Since the weather was a little chilly that morning, Brenda had decided to leave her two children at home. The younger of her children, Shantell, was still nursing a severe cold and her older brother Reggie showed symptoms of coming down with one. Usually Brenda would drag them along with her, but not this day.

"Sorry, baby, I can't take you with me today. When you get better, you can come."

"Mommy, I'm alright. I feel good," Shantell countered. "There's nothing wrong with me no more. My cold is all gone."

Look, I don't care what you say. I'm your mother, and what I say, goes," Brenda reiterated. "Next time."

Brenda went to her son's bedroom. She found him playing video games on the television.

"Reggie, look after your sister. I'm getting ready to go now. I'll be back in a few hours, Jehovah willing."

"Why I always gotta watch her? Can't you take her with you?" Reggie complained.

"No, I can't take her with me," Brenda barked. "You watching her because I said so."

"Shoot, I'm sick of this house. I wanna go back to live with my father," he fired back. "Every time I turn around, I gotta baby-sit. I'm getting tired of that. All you do is run down to the Kingdom Hall and do field service. You do all the praying in the world and that still ain't getting us nowhere. We still right here in the projects."

By anyone's standards Reggie was a problem child, or the black sheep of the family. He stayed in trouble constantly. Reggie had been rebellious before, during and after Brenda's religious conversion. Reggie had one hell of a mouth on him. Brenda always said her son was Fourteen going on forty.

At that point Brenda could have slapped her son's head off, she was that mad. Suddenly she remembered her religious beliefs and that seemed to quell her anger.

Shantell stood in the hallway, listening to her mother and older brother go at it. They exchanged heated words back and forth. It was as if Shantell wasn't even there. She couldn't help but feel that their argument was over her. Their conversation made her feel unwanted.

"Shut up!" Brenda commanded. "I don't wanna hear another doggone word come out your mouth. All that talk is devilment."

Reggie sucked his teeth and went back to playing his video game. Quietly, his mother backed out of the room. She went downstairs with Shantell following close behind.

As Brenda reached the front door, she turned back toward her daughter. She scooped Shantell up in her arms and embraced her.

"I'll see you later," Brenda said. "Be good for Mommy. Don't give your brother no trouble, okay?"

"Okay, Mommy," Shantell replied. "I won't."

Reggie stood at the top of the stairs looking down at the scene and it made him furious. This was the stuff he was talking about. He always felt that his sister, Shantell, got preferential treatment. He thought that his sister was his mother's favorite child. To him, it seemed like he could do no right in her eyes. Reggie felt like an outsider in his own family. He went back to his room, feeling miserable.

"Bye." Brenda said, as she closed the door behind her.

A small tear ran down Shantell's cheek. She hated being at home alone with her brother. All he did was boss her around and pick on her. She never could understand why he would do this to her. After all, Shantell never did anything to him; nothing to deserve this kind of treatment. Reggie was just mean and nasty toward her for no reason other than he could.

Shantell decided to stir clear of her brother. She would simply stay in her room, till her mother returned home. That was her best bet if she wanted to avoid Reggie's wrath. Her brother was a tyrant when no one was around.

Silently she crept upstairs undetected. Closing her room door, she busied herself playing a game of jacks. The game of jacks was a childhood favorite of Shantell's. It allowed her to play with other people or by herself; usually, it was the later. The game didn't require much to play, just a small, bouncy ball, ten metal jacks, a smooth surface, and good timing.

Shantell was totally engrossed in the game. She played it over and over again and never seemed to get tired. It was fun to her. Playing jacks alone in her room by herself beat dealing with her brother any day.

"Yeah, I won." Shantell cried.

As the morning wore on, Shantell began to physically tire. She decided to take a nap. Hopefully, when she awoke her mother would be home and all her problems would be solved. The minute her head touched the pillow, she was asleep. When Shantell slept, she was hard to wake.

The absence of noise in the house made Reggie suspicious. He had already shut off his play station video game system. He wished he had some new games because he was tired of playing the ones he had. He got up and began to creep around the house.

He went straight to his sister's room. He wanted to see exactly what she was doing. Maybe he would mess with her, since he had nothing better to do.

Reggie and Shantell were half brother and sister; they had the same mother but different fathers. To him, half of a sister was like no sister at all. Shantell was fair game. She was subject to whatever twisted scenario he thought up.

Both of their dads were deadbeats, good for nothing, although Reggie's father was a little bit better than Shantell's. Though he hadn't come around since his son was a baby, at least He did send financial support from time to time. When the money came, Brenda divided it between both of her kids. She took care of both Reggie and Shantell the best way she could, even if that meant robbing Peter to pay Paul.

Quietly, Reggie stuck his head through her bedroom door. He was surprised to find Shantell asleep. Immediately, Reggie's devious mind went to work. Forever the prankster, Reggie thought about giving his sister a hot foot. He laughed to himself as he envisioned her jumping out of bed with her toes on fire, then he dismiss the idea. Reggie remembered he had already done that. Over the years he had really done some cruel things to Shantell. A devilish thought crept into Reggie's mind. Now he was about to outdo himself. What he was about to do was to commit a crime against humanity.

Shantell rested peacefully on her twin bed, sound asleep on her back. There was no way in the world she could have been aware of what was about to happen next.

There were more than a few incidents that led up this dastardly deed. Reggie had inappropriately touched her on several occasions. He even burst into the bathroom while she was in the shower once. Shantell's innocence prevented her from correctly assessing the situation. Letting him get away with this would prove to be the biggest mistake of her life.

Carefully Reggie climbed atop Shantell. He was cautious not to put his entire body weight on her. Shantell didn't move a muscle, she was sound asleep. With one hand he pinned both her arms above her head and to the bed. With the other hand, he clawed at her pajama bottom.

Now Shantell was wide awake. There was a confused look in her eyes as she looked up at her brother. She wondered what he was doing. Reggie had done some crazy things in the past, but he had never played with her like this.

"Get off me!" She yelled. "What you doing? I'm telling Mommy."

Only a divine act of intervention would save Shantell from this beastly act. She would never need her mother more in her life than she needed her now.

Shantell's cries for help would go unanswered. Her brother had a wild look in his eye, as if he was if were high, but he wasn't. He was just evil. He was just determined to violate her. He didn't give a fuck about her and this was his way of showing it.

"Shut the fuck up!" He barked through clenched teeth. "Shut up, bitch, 'fore I kill you."

Shantell didn't listen to him. She kept on screaming.

Suddenly Reggie stopped right in the middle of his act, wrapped both of his hands around Shantell's neck, and began choking her. Desperately, she tried to fight him off. She feared that he would make good on his promise and kill her. Her blows had little or no effect on Reggie. He continued to strangle her.

Shantell's face turned beet red from lack of oxygen. She began to lose consciousness. Just as she did so, Reggie came to his senses and released his grip. He had succeeded in taking all the fight out of his sister. She coughed and choked repeatedly, trying to fill her lungs with air.

With Shantell rendered defenseless, Reggie began to have his way with her. He pulled her pants and panties off, and then he tried to insert his penis inside of her vagina.

Shantell's vagina was tighter than that of any girl Reggie's age; after all, she was still a child. Still, Reggie was determined to penetrate her. He didn't feel a bit of remorse, either. After several failed attempts, he finally succeeded in reaching his goal. Reggie humped his young sister with reckless abandon.

Reggie's sexual invasion of his sister's body was an unbearable moment for Shantell. Her young body was suddenly filled with excruciating pain. She cried out as if she were mortally wounded.

Shantell's cries of pain only excited him. Her pain bought him joy. Within minutes it was over and Reggie had ejaculated inside her. He picked himself up and fastened his pants.

Shantell just lay there, momentarily frozen. The blank stare in her eyes suggested she was in a different place. This was an outer-body experience.

"Get yo' ass up, girl, and get in the shower," Reggie ordered. "Hurry up 'fore Mommy come home."

Ignoring her brother's command, Shantell didn't move. Reggie repeated himself again. Once again, his sister didn't respond.

He reached down and snatched his half-naked sister off the bed, then slammed Shantell up against the wall. Her bible study plaques and Double Dutch trophies fell from the wall and dresser. Reggie brought his face inches from hers. Then he spoke in low menacing voice.

"Listen, you little bitch, you better do what I say," he growled. "And you better not tell nobody what we did! You hear me? If you do, I am going to kill you!"

In reality, Shantell had nothing to fear. Reggie could not hurt her anymore than he already had. Right now, she was already dead. He couldn't possibly kill her again.

His harsh words began to invoke tears from Shantell eyes. She cried uncontrollably. Her whole body began to tremble. She was scared to death of her brother.

Reggie did more than intimidate Shantell. He instilled the fear of God in her. She really believed he would carry out his threat. Shantell really thought her brother was crazy. Suddenly she began to do what she was told.

Evilly Reggie looked at her as she exited the room. When Shantell was out of sight, he went over and inspected the bed. He saw a few light blood stains on the sheets. Immediately he tore the sheets off the bed and flipped the mattress over. He went down the hall to the linen closet and got a fresh set of sheets in an effort to cover his tracks, and put them on Shantell's bed, as if his mother had made it up. Brenda had taught her son well.

Reggie hid the soiled sheets in his bedroom until later. As soon as he got the opportunity, he planned to dispose of the evidence in the project Dumpster. Until then, Reggie retreated back to his room to play his video game. He acted as if nothing ever happened.

He figured even if Shantell did tell, it would be his word against hers. Who would Brenda believe? Reggie would make his mother choose sides. That was something that no parent wanted to do under any conditions.

Meanwhile, inside the bathroom, the shower water constantly ran. Shantell lay balled up on the floor near the bathtub. She was overcome by a sickening feeling. She wasn't sure exactly what happened but she knew it wasn't right. After awhile, Shantell pulled herself together long enough to take a shower.

In every person's life there is that event or situation that defines the rest of there life. It either helps or hinders them. For Shantell Bryant, this was it. After this incident, life would be a game of catch up. Her mental growth would be forever stagnated.

Shantell would never again be the same. She would never be that innocent little girl again. Never.

❧❧❧

As the years passed, Shantell never broke her silence. She never told a soul, including her mother, what happened in her bedroom on that fateful day. Reggie repaid her for her silence by continuing to sexually assault her at every opportunity he got. He turned his sister into his own personal whore.

Shantell quickly became submissive to her brother's strong sexual urges. Each time they had sex, it became easier and easier for him to take advantage of her. He forced her to anything and everything he could think of sexually.

Brenda Bryant's life seemed to unravel simultaneously with her daughter's. She found out that breaking old drug habits was hard to do. Her crack cocaine habit resurfaced with a vengeance. Brenda went on drug binges, disappearing for days at a time. Soon, her crack habit began to grow out of control.

She began to steal from her employers, who subsequently fired her. They didn't press charges on her because of all the years of loyal service. Her drug addition took precedence over everything, God included. The Kingdom Hall and the Jehovah's Witnesses became an afterthought. She had a new religion; it was called addiction and her Higher Power was crack. She prayed to her cocaine god daily. Brenda turned her back on everything that she loved. She was in no position to help herself, never mind Shantell. Her life was slowly spiraling down the drain of life.

❧❧

By the time Shantell reached her teens, she was a young black girl lost. She began acting out. It started out by skipping classes at school. When she reached high school, she stopped going all together. She would pick fights with her mother over the smallest things, like what Brenda was cooking for dinner.

Drugs had broken the tight bond that they once shared, blinding Brenda to her daughter's problems. Drugs had deafened Brenda's ears to Shantell's pleas for help.

Without the proper guidance of a parent, Shantell was free to roam the projects aimlessly. It didn't take long for the neighborhood boys to figure her out and have sex with her, and she was labeled "easy."

Bouncing from house to house seemed to mold Shantell. She seemed to learn from every sexual situation she was in. Her trials and tribulations would evolve her into the cold, heartless bitch she would later become.

After the sexual romps with her brother, whenever she got into one-on-one, intimate situations with the opposite sex, Shantell was afraid to tell the guy no; thoughts of her brother would flash through her mind. She remembered the way he used to hit her and threaten her if she turned away his sexual advances. So to avoid any confrontations, she just said yes. She figured that if she gave them what they wanted, then she could get rid of them that much faster.

Before long, older predators and pedophiles in the projects were drawn to Shantell's beauty like a vulture to a dead, rotting carcass. They began to take advantage of her, too. Sometimes, it wasn't always the men who were the guilty party. In this new world the women were just as dangerous.

"Knock, Knock."
"Who is it?" A female voice shouted.
"It's me, Shantell," she replied.
Suddenly the door swung open and Shantell was granted entrance. "Come in," said a voice from behind the door. "Hurry up." Immediately Shantell recognized the voice as that of her friend Keisha's older sister, Brandy. She was partially clothed, which explained why she was hiding behind the door. Once Shantell was safely inside the house, Brandy shut the door behind her. Now Brandy revealed her half-dressed body. She was wearing a pretty white lace panty-and-bra set. It really seemed to enhance her sex appeal, and the color brought out her caramel completion. Where Keisha at?" Shantell asked.

"Keisha ain't here." Brandy announced. "She went over to the mall real quick. She said she be right back."

"Damn, why she ain't call me and tell me that," Shantell said. "I coulda stayed home."

"You can wait for her here." Brandy assured her. "She'll be right back. What you got better to do? I thought y'all were going out to the movies?"

Brandy was right; what did she have better to do? There was no way she was going back home. Lately she hated to be inside her house longer than necessary. Shantell just slept there. She began to despise not only her brother, but her mother too. Once she left her house, she stayed gone.

What Shantell didn't know was that she was being set up. Her friend Keisha had traded her sister a pair of new sneakers, for time alone with Shantell. Brandy was bisexual and strongly attracted to Shantell. She had been begging her younger sister for a crack at her friend. Finally Keisha had relented, only after Brandy had given her some money to buy the latest Jordan's.

"Come upstairs to my room," Brandy called out. "It's cool. I'm up here watching videos on BET."

The ploy seemed to work. Shantell followed Brandy up the stairs to her bedroom. As she did, she couldn't help but notice that Brandy's ass cheeks hung outside her panties. There wasn't enough material to cover her completely.

Brandy began to sway her hips, knowing Shantell was watching. She hoped that would entice her. Unfortunately for Brandy, Shantell didn't show any emotion either way.

As soon as they entered the room, Brandy turned around and stepped to her business. She grabbed Shantell and pulled her close. She looked her dead in the eyes and began to French kiss her. Once Shantell didn't protest, Brandy knew she had her. She turned into an octopus; to Shantell, her hands seemed to be everywhere. They groped Shantell's private parts and breasts, while at the same time undressing her.

Soon they stood in the middle of the room, completely naked. By this time, Shantell had begun to reciprocate Brandy's sexual advances. They continued to kiss. A strange feeling was overcoming her, and she liked it.

Shantell liked the sweet aroma of a woman. She liked the soft touch of a woman's hands and her body. She liked what was going on right now. A man had never made her feel this good.

Brandy was loving life right now. The fact that Shantell had responded to her sexual advances, turned her on even more. To her, there was nothing like wanting somebody and them wanting you back. As Shantell's reactions increased, it intensified Brandy's passion. She pulled Shantell to the floor so she could really get down to business.

Once on the floor, Brandy buried her face inside Shantell's pussy. She licked, sucked, and fingered Shantell's clit. Shantell began to lift her ass off the floor to meet Brandy's hungry mouth. Shantell was in a sexual trance. This wasn't the first time she had gotten her pussy eaten, but it was by far the best. She found out first hand that nobody could please a woman like another woman could.

Shantell began to go into sexual convulsions. Her lips quivered as she climaxed time after time. Brandy was unrelenting; she kept right on doing her thing. She was trying to make this something Shantell would never forget. She was trying to turn her out.

What Brandy really did that day was add to the confusion already going on in Shantell's life. She had Shantell questioning her own sexuality. Was she gay, straight or bisexual? What Shantell really was, was confused.

Brandy had succeeded in seducing Shantell. She uttered the magical words, "I love you." No one outside of Shantell's mother had ever told Shantell that. Shantell believed Brandy because she wanted to be loved. Better yet, Shantell needed to be loved, regardless of whatever form love came in. To her, love was love.

Shantell was at Brandy's beck and call. After awhile, the newness of the relationship began to wear off. Brandy did what every other sexual partner, in the past had done to Shantell. She passed her off to someone else.

"Lonnie, get over here quick!" Brandy whispered into the phone. "I got something for you. Nigga, you gone like this."

"It's about time, you hadn't hooked a nigga up in a minute," he exclaimed. "Gimme fifteen minutes. I'll be right there."

Lonnie was a world-class hustler from Piedmont Court. He and Brandy had twisted a lot of chicks out together on many occasions. Or, whenever one of them was tired of a sex partner, they passed them off to the other.

Before Brandy knew it, Lonnie was knocking at her back door. As he stepped inside the house Brandy put a finger to her lips in order to silence him. She could tell that Lonnie was overexcited, maybe a bit over anxious. He knew this had to be good. Brandy wouldn't call him for nothing.

"Yo, what's up with this be quiet shit?" he asked. "I ain't got time for all this. I gotta be somewhere. Let me do me, so I can go."

"Would you calm down for minute and let me tell you the deal," she insisted. "Now listen, all you gotta do is…"

Brandy instructed Lonnie on how to go about every-thing. This was a delicate situation; if it was handled wrong, then it could mean a rape charge for somebody. Once Brandy put him down with the situation, Lonnie knew he had to use some finesse. After awhile, Lonnie began to have second thoughts about things. He sent Brandy in his place to make sure everything was a go.

Inside the bedroom, Shantell lay on the bed covered by only a white sheet. Brandy walked in and immediately joined her. After a few passionate kisses, Brandy popped the question.

"Shantell, you know I love you, right?"

"Yeah, I know," Shantell replied.

"Well, listen…I got this friend sitting' in the living room. I need you to do me a favor. I need you to take care of him for me. Alright?"

If Shantell ever thought that Brandy loved her or even cared for her, she now knew it wasn't true. Brandy had sold her out just like everyone else, just when she was at a vulnerable point in her life.

"Wait right here. I'm going to send him in."

The instant Lonnie laid eyes on Shantell, he got excited. The girl was pretty, young, and in shape. That was a deadly combination in his eyes. He stripped off his clothes and pro-ceeded to have sex with Shantell.

During the course of their sexual encounter, Shantell was so wet, that Lonnie's condom had slipped off without him even knowing. He was horrified to make that discovery after he ejaculated inside Shantell. It was too late; there was nothing he could do about it.

After Brandy had passed Shantell off to Lonnie, she began to have second thoughts about her. Shantell became soured on the idea of having a relationship with Brandy. Soon, they went their separate ways.

❧

As Shantell struggled with her sexuality, her brother had problems of his own. The black cloud that surrounded Piedmont Courts had engulfed Reggie too. He had fallen in with an older crowd; a group of stick-up kids to be specific. They had been using Reggie as a fall guy. They had him commit the crimes they wouldn't dare do.

Since Reggie looked up to them, he had no problem putting a gun in his hand and robbing people. He had robbed almost every Circle K gas station in the city twice. Pictures of Reggie began to appear on the nightly news and on some city billboards. His days as a free man were numbered. It was another crime that ultimately would become Reggie's undoing.

Returning home from a failed robbery attempt, Reggie decided to rob the taxicab driver who had driven him home. The robbery turned into a homicide when the cab driver resisted. Reggie blew the African man's brains out.

This senseless killing had appalled an entire city. Law enforcement authorities had put a lot of heat on the street. Eventually one of their snitches gave up Reggie's name. Previously, he had been overheard bragging about the crime in the projects.

Late at night, the S.W.A.T. team raided the Bryant home and found the murder weapon. Neither Shantell nor her mother was home at the time. The case was open and shut.

Reggie Bryant was tried and convicted. He was sentenced to life imprisonment.

There was one person in the world who didn't feel sorry for Reggie. That was his sister, Shantell. She thought that her brother had gotten what he deserved. She called it karma. She was glad he was gone; maybe now she could get her life on track.

In the months that followed her brother's arrest, Shantell discovered she was pregnant. The fact that she was going to be teenage mom didn't even worry her. She always wanted to have something or someone to love unconditionally; now she would have that in the form of a child.

Of all the young lives that were forever altered by circumstances beyond their control in Piedmont Courts, none would change more drastically than Shantell Bryant's.

CHAPTER 3
You're a big girl now

The warm spring sunlight felt good against Shantell's skin. It was a picture perfect day in Charlotte, North Carolina. The nice weather wasn't what brought her outside on this day. The reason she was out at mid-day was opportunity. She desperately needed the opportunity to make some quick money. Even more so, Shantell needed the opportunity to provide for her infant daughter.

It was no secret in Piedmont Courts that Shantell was damaged goods. She had been around the block more than a few times. So any questions of paternity were bound to invoke anger from any suspecting male. They all claimed, "It ain't mine." Another favorite was, "What you telling me for?" Shantell contacted guy after guy, but no one would man up. Some guys even went so far as to threaten to do bodily harm to her. Nobody wanted their reputation tarnished by having a baby by a hoe or a freak.

The entire ordeal was enough to break Shantell's spirits, yet she refused to fold. If no one would own up to being her child's father, then she wouldn't make them. She wouldn't take a bunch of dude's downtown to the white man just to figure out the paternity. She wasn't about to bring three or four possible baby daddies on a talk show, either, only to hear" You are *not* the father!" No, Shantell would spare herself any further embarrassment. From here on out, this was between her, Jordan and God.

Shantell decided to put an "H" on her chest and handle it. She would be both the child's mother and father. She would show these niggers that she was more of a man than they would ever be. *Fuck them all*, she thought.

the interim, Shantell went downtown to the welfare agency, applied for and received public assistance. She applied for Section Eight, low-income housing and was placed on a waiting list. Shantell applied for the works; whatever she could get, she was going to get. Still, she wouldn't sit back and depend on the government to take care of her child. Shantell was about to take matters into her own hands.

The birth of her daughter had succeeded in doing one thing, if nothing else: it succeeded in getting Shantell to become more serious and more focused about life. She had no choice but to get out and get it. Life had never given Shantell Bryant anything except the blues, so she didn't expect anything from it to now.

❧❧

The birth of her new baby, Jordan, had given Shantell a set of newfound responsibilities. Babies had needs and those needs had to be met.

The Club Champagne was located on Atando Avenue, just off North Tryon Street. It was housed in an average-sized, pale white, non-descript building. Nothing about the place suggested luxury; by no means was this place classy or upscale. On the contrary, it was as hood as it gets. Still, it was a hotspot, renowned throughout the city. It was a known fact that any stripper that was about anything danced here at one time or another.

Shantell stood against the powder white wall, relaxing. She wasn't too concerned with getting dirty. She was just trying to stay out of the sun. Periodically, Shantell checked her wrist watch; she anxiously awaited the club's manager, Tommy. She wanted to get this over and done with. It seemed that she was a little early. When one depended on public transportation to get around, it was best to be early than to be late. In the hood, it seemed like city buses came when they wanted to. There was no rhyme or reason to their schedules.

As Shantell looked around the desolate block, she noticed another young woman approaching. She would bet her last dollar that the young woman was coming to the exact same place. One didn't have to be a psychic to figure that out. There was nothing else around, except warehouses and factories.

"Hey," the young lady spoke. "You been waiting here long?"

Shantell replied, "Not that long."

Shantell wasn't big on talking to strangers; she was a loner. She had trouble trusting people. She preferred to keep it brief when dealing with them. She only spoke when spoken to, and she didn't volunteer any information. It was a tough task trying to get Shantell to engage in a conversation.

For some reason, the young lady didn't take hints well. She continued to attempt to strike up a conversation, which turned out to be one-sided in her favor.

"You auditioning today huh? Where you from? What's your name? How old are you? You got kids?" The girl continued to pester her.

Though Shantell didn't particularly care to talk, the girl almost forced the words out of Shantell's mouth with her in-depth line of questions. Against her better judgment, Shantell began to take a liking to the girl.

"Damn, you sure ask a lot of questions," Shantell hinted. "And I don't even know yo' name?"

The young lady's smile deflected any signs of hostility that may have been in the air. She was thick skinned with a good sense of humor. Dee-Dee felt like if she talked to anybody long enough, she would make them like her. Dee-Dee thought she was so likable, even the Klan would like her. Dee-Dee knew she could be a pest at times; that was the only knock against her.

If she befriended you, though, one had a friend to the end. A fair-weather friend she wasn't.

"My bad! My name is Denise. Denise Daniels. But everybody calls me Dee-Dee."

"Well, Dee-Dee, meet Shantell," she announced. "How the hell are you?"

Shantell straightened up and offered the girl a handshake. Dee-Dee accepted and Shantell leaned back up against the wall. There, she was comfortable and content. From her position on the wall, Shantell proceeded to answer all of Dee-Dee's questions; plus, she managed to sneak in a few of her own. Before the two women knew it, they had begun to click. Shantell found out that Dee-Dee's background was similar to hers. They both came from the hood, and each had faced adversity in different ways.

While they talked Shantell gave Dee-Dee the once-over. She had to admit that Dee-Dee had the goods. She was tall but not lanky. She stood approximately 5'10" with short hair, big bubbly eyes, and a mind-blowing body. Every part of Dee-Dee was big, butt her body came together nicely; each part complimented the other. The amazing thing about her was she was elegant, not clumsy. She carried herself very well. Shantell was impressed by her beauty and the way she carried herself. She gave credit where it was due.

From out of nowhere, a black Mercedes Benz S500 suddenly appeared. As it pulled into the small makeshift parking lot, all conversation ceased between the girls. All eyes were on the beautiful foreign sedan and its occupant. The girls were almost certain that this was Tommy, the club's owner, manager, crisis counselor and anything else one could think of. Who else could it be, pulling up to a strip club early in the afternoon?

Tommy was a hustler from the old school. He had made his money and his mark on the streets of Charlotte, way before these two were even born. Well into his forties, Tommy was old enough to be both these girls' father; and the way he spread himself around, he quite possibly could be.

The thing Tommy never did was mix business with pleasure. He never had sex with the strippers who worked for him. He knew if he did that, then they would lose all respect. They would never follow his orders. In their minds, he would be no different from any other trick in the club. Strippers were some very strange characters. In order to keep his operation running smoothly, Tommy made money with the strippers and fucked elsewhere.

First and foremost, Tommy was about that dollar. He was always looking for that fresh face, or a young chick to add new blood to the club. In the strip club scene, old was bad and new was good. Who was Tommy to buck that trend? It was a time-tested theory for every strip joint in the country. It worked time and time again. There was nothing an old trick loved more than a new hoe.

"Sorry I'm late," he stated. "I had to make a little run to the other side of town and everything. I hope y'all can forgive me. I appreciate y'all waiting for me."

"No problem," Dee-Dee answered.

Tommy was a big man powerfully built. He had thick arms and a broad chest. He stood 6'4" and weighed in at 260 pounds. He had an imposing physical presence about him that seemed to demand respect from everyone. Tommy wasn't the type one would want to bump into in a dark alley. He crushed gravel beneath his feet as he walked toward the door. He was a heavyweight in every sense of the word.

He quickly undid the lock to the club, opened the door, and deactivated the security alarm. The girls followed him right in. Even when he flipped on the lights, the club was still dim; there was just enough light to see. From the looks of things, someone had been cleaning up last night. The chairs were atop the tables and the countertops of the bar were clean.

"Follow me," he said. "We going back to my office."

The girls did just what they were told. His office was right behind the counter.

The lighting in the office was a lot better. Now Tommy could see exactly what he was getting. One look at these two and he knew he had two winners. If he didn't know outside, he knew now. Mentally, Tommy kicked himself; he wished he had one of his partners there with him to see what he was about to see. He would have called them but there was no time for that.

"The show must go on," he thought.

The office was small but it was nicely furnished with a desktop computer, printer and monitor. There was also a large wooden desk and three chairs. Tommy sat behind the desk and reclined in a leather chair, looking every bit like the boss he was.

"Alright, ladies. I guess you know what you're here for? Correct?"

"Yeah," Dee-Dee replied.

"How about you?" He looked at Shantell. "You ain't said two words yet. You alright?"

Tommy was concerned by Shantell's lack of verbal communication. This business wasn't for the timid or weak. Only the strong survived here. He had seen the strip club chew up and spit out so many weak strippers. Before one knew it, they were either full-fledged prostitutes or strung out on drugs. One had to be strong to handle the day-to-day bullshit that went on in the club. Taking your clothes off in front of complete strangers, without any shame, wasn't normal at all.

Auditioning the girls was Tommy's way of weeding out the weak. It didn't do him any good to have a stripper quit on him in the middle of a packed house. If a potential stripper couldn't cut it here, in his office, then she certainly couldn't cut it later. So why waste his time or theirs? Tommy was going to cut straight to the chase right now.

"I'm alright," Shantell admitted. "Don't mind me. I ain't too much on talking."

"Well, we gotta get you up outta that bad habit. That ain't good for business, yours or mine. You understand?"

"Oh, don't worry. I'll talk when I have to. I'm about my business. Believe me," Shantell assured him. "It's not a problem."

"Okay, okay. That's what I like to hear. I was just checking."

A sly smile creased his lips in anticipation was what was to come. This wasn't an expression of approval; it was one of pure lust.

"Oh, yeah! I just remembered something. Ladies, could I see some ID, please? The law requires that you young ladies be at least eighteen. And I ain't trying to spend a day in jail for nobody! We'll have none of that underage shit in here. The Man will run up in here and shut us down quick, fast, and in a hurry."

The girls reached into their respective purses and handed over the proper credentials. Tommy scrutinized both of their North Carolina state-issued identifications.

"Shantell?" he called out.

"Yeah, that's me," she replied.

"And you must be Denise?"

"All day, every day," Dee-Dee chimed.

On his computer, Tommy scanned a copy of both their identifications, for his personal records, before he gave them back Now the fun part was about to begin.

"Here y'all go," he began. "If y'all wouldn't mind, would y'all take off y'all's clothes?"

The girls rose from their seats and did what was asked of them. Tommy could hardly contain himself as he watched with earnest. He was a sexual freak in every sense of the word. All he could think about was giving the young girls oral sex, right here and right now. He examined the duo so closely; he should have been a gynecologist.

In no time they were butt naked, standing right in front of him. Each woman possessed a killer body. They both had the physical traits that Tommy liked in his women. Dee-Dee had the fat ass that Tommy required of any woman he was sleeping with. Shantell, on the other hand, was slim in the waist and pretty in the face. The absence of body fat really turned him on. He would have bit his lip at the sight of these two naked, but it would have seemed very unprofessional. Though he saw gorgeous bodies every day of the week, these two were the exception to the rule. The *crème de la crème*.

Tommy's first impression of Shantell was that she was exceptionally beautiful and unusually poised. If this was her first time stripping in front of a stranger, he couldn't tell.

All the sex that Shantell had had over the years had broken her out of her shyness. She didn't hesitate when given an instruction, nor did she squirm under close examination. Every step of the way, she proved that she had whatever it took to work there, and so did Dee-Dee. They were only young in age, not experience.

"Alright, ladies could both of y'all spin around and shake what your momma gave y'all? Dance!" I usually make girls do this to music, but I ain't got none. So y'all gonna have to use your imagination."

The girls danced as if there was music in the room. Their timing seemed to be in sync to the imaginary beat. Tommy watched as their asses jiggled and wiggled. The girls grinded their hips and dropped it like it was hot. After seeing that, the girls finally got Tommy's seal of approval.

"Goddamn!" he exclaimed. "You two make a nigger wish he was young again. For real! I bullshit you not!"

With that comment, Tommy had cosigned for them. They were officially strippers. He liked what he saw.

"Oh, before I forget, let me ask you young ladies a serious question. Do any of you have a husband, boyfriend, or significant other? Basically what I'm asking is, is there any jealous-ass or pussy-whooped nigger that might have a problem with either one of you dancing in here?"

Tommy's latest question probably was the most important thing he would ever ask because if either of their answers were yes, then he couldn't employ them. He didn't want any parts of domestic drama around his place of business. Violence wasn't good for any business.

"No!" they both seemed to say in unison.

"Okay, just checking. 'Cause niggers act a fool over some pussy that may not even be theirs. Another thing: there's no drinking alcohol while on the job."

As the girls got dressed, Tommy went on to explain the club rules and the code of conduct. He became a little repetitive because he wanted to be clear. The rules were the rules; break them and you were gone. He would personally give you your walking papers. Certain things would not be tolerated by Tommy, regardless of who you were or how good you looked. You violated the rules, you were gone. It was that simple.

"Look, y'all be here tonight. Nine o'clock sharp!"

❧❧

Later that night, Jordan, curled up in Shantell's lap. She gently stroked her daughter's hair. In so many ways, Shantell was comforting her. Through the sense of touch, Shantell conveyed to Jordan that she was here for her and always would be. The toddler desperately tried to fight sleep, but to no avail. The feeling was too good. Sleep was slowly overcoming her, anyway. The baby began to play with her own ear. This was a sign to Shantell that her daughter would be fast asleep shortly. The sooner she went to sleep, the better, because Shantell had to be at work in a little while.

Shantell gently placed her daughter on the bed. As soon as she did, the phone rang loudly in her room. She reached for it to keep it from waking her baby.

"Hello?" she whispered.

"You have a collect call from…" an automated voice began.

Shantell didn't need to hear any more of the recording. She knew who the caller was and where the person was calling from. Angrily, she hung up on the caller.

"Fuck you! Motherfucker!" She cursed. "I hope ya' dumb ass rots in jail. Die slow, bitch!"

The caller was none other than her brother Reggie, who was currently serving a life sentence in a remote North Carolina prison. Now that Shantell had the upper hand she was doing Reggie dirty, just like he had done her. Every letter that came from the prison to the house, she tore up and threw it away. Every time Reggie called, she hung up on him. Shantell planned on getting a block placed on the phone so Reggie couldn't call any more. She knew the reason why he was calling: Reggie was in need. If Shantell had her way, then her brother would be doing hard time for the rest of his life. In her mind, he deserved every day he got and more.

Shantell would never forgive her brother for what he had done to her, nor would she forget. What he did was inexcusable, in her mind. She was glad he was in prison. Her mind often drifted to him when she was alone. She often thought about how her life may have been different, had he not have raped her. Had he not stripped her of something she could never get back: her innocence.

Shantell never sat back feeling sorry for herself, though. She rolled with the punches that life had thrown at her. Not once did she complain.

Shantell was disturbed by the call. She went around the house and disconnected every phone line. In her book, Reggie didn't exist anymore. She still had a lot of hatred and animosity toward her mother and brother.

"Ma?" Shantell called out.

Shantell crept out of her room and down the hall toward her mother's bedroom. After taking a few steps, she suddenly came to halt.

"Owww!" she screamed. "What the hell is that on the floor?"

Shantell had just stepped on some foreign object. She looked down to see the source of her pain. She turned her foot over and picked an empty vial of crack off the sole of her foot.

"Damn, this bitch is outta control," she said aloud. "I don't believe this shit. I gotta get outta here."

Tossing the drug paraphernalia aside, she went to her mother's bedroom door. The door was closed but Shantell didn't bother to knock; she walked right on in.

"Ma?" She announced before stopping in her tracks.

Brenda Bryant was caught red-handed. The crack pipe was at her lips and the ever-present stench of crack smoke was in the air. Shantell couldn't believe her eyes; there was undeniable evidence everywhere, in plain view. There were empty crack vials on the dresser and burnt matches galore.

Shantell watched her mother free-basing and instantly became sick. To know she was getting high was one thing, but to see it was something else. She was repulsed by the sight.

Brenda merely turned her head towards her daughter, acknowledging her presence. Not once did she stop what she was doing. She saw no reason to. She wasn't the least bit ashamed.

"What the hell are you doing?" Shantell asked, as if she didn't know. "Look at you! You high as a kite. I'm not leaving my baby here with you and you all high."

Brenda would have protested but all the cocaine in her system had rendered her speechless. She just stared wide-eyed at her daughter.

Shantell continued, "You need some fucking help! Bad! Just look at you. You don't care about nothing or no one!"

Shantell went back to her room and made a series of phone calls. She called all around Piedmont Courts looking for a reliable baby sitter. She was in luck. Shantell found a friend of a friend to keep her baby. Shantell dressed Jordan and carried her just a few doors away. Now that her baby was situated, she could now go about her business of making them some money.

Shantell went back home and gathered up the things she would need for tonight and place them in a small duffle bag. Then she called her ride, Dee-Dee, to come pick her up.

For the first time in a long time, Shantell felt good about her future prospects. She felt like she was on the fast track to some real money. It was too bad that the fast track she was on led to nowhere, fast.

❧❦

The neon lights above the building were ablaze, the sign read Club Champagne. To Shantell, it didn't look much different than it had in the daytime except now; even a casual observer knew what kind of club this was. This was the kind where memberships weren't required to gain entrance. The kind where money was all you needed to have a good time.

Shantell and Dee-Dee arrived at the Club Champagne a little after nine 'o clock. They were so early that there were only a handful of cars in the parking lot. The only signs of life they saw were two stocky security guards, worked diligently at setting up barriers. The club expected a large turnout of male customers tonight.

The girls thought they had made a mistake of arriving at the club too early. They forgot that all the real hustlers and ballers don't really start to come out until eleven thirty or twelve o'clock. Whether it was a party or a strip club, the same rules applied. They knew niggers always came late. They can't ever be on time for nothing, not even their own funeral.

The young women stepped out of a late model, gold, four-door Mazda Protégé. Shantell's duffle bag sat between her legs while Dee-Dee's sat on the back seat. After Shantell retrieved her bag, they began to walk towards the entrance. They managed to navigate the treacherous parking lot terrain, which consisted of loose gravel and dust, in high-heeled shoes. They thought about falling with every step.

It was safe to say that they wouldn't ever make the mistake of wearing high heels to the club again. Both Shantell and Dee-Dee didn't have a clue of just what they were in for tonight. They would have to walk around all night in these same shoes. At some point during the night, they would find that task unbearable.

"Remember, my name is So Sexy," Shantell reminded Dee-Dee. "And your name is Baby Cakes."

"Alright, I got it," Dee-Dee replied. "You don't gotta tell me twice. I'm real good with names."

With that said, they entered the club. The place was now very much alive. Loud rap music blared from the club's sound system. A few scantily clad strippers milled around the bar area, fraternizing with the patrons. After taking a few blind steps deeper into the club, they were suddenly greeted by Tommy.

"Good to see you could join us," He commented. "Follow me this way, and I'll show you around."

Tommy took the girls on a brief tour of the club. He introduced them to everybody they needed to know in the club, from the bartender to the bouncers. After a brief discussion, he led them to the dressing room.

Shantell and Dee-Dee quickly got dressed or undressed, however one wanted to look at it. Either way, they changed into more revealing outfits. Shantell slipped into an ultra tight, two-piece outfit. The halter top with the matching micro mini-skirt called attention to her ass cheeks. Since she was short, Shantell wore clear seven–inch, open-toed platform shoes. Dee-Dee's outfit consisted of a hot pink bikini with matching booty shorts that looked like a pair of thongs on her, because her ass was so big. She topped that off with sexy five-inch sandals with tie-up strings that wrapped around her legs. They exuded sex appeal in every sense of the word. Once that was done, they secured their belongings in a locker and hit the club.

It was a brave new world inside the Club Champagne once one makes that transition from "regular chick" to "stripper." Now everyone looked at them differently. In this world, it was high risk and high reward. The more things a stripper was prepared to do, the more money she stood to make. The club may have had strict rules but once the doors of the club closed, it was anything goes.

The girls tried hard to blend into the scenery. The strange stares went unreturned. Shantell had no illusions or reservations about stripping; she was here to do what she had to do to get that money. As soon as she hit the floor, she went to work.

Shantell didn't know about Dee-Dee, but she had a plan. She wasn't going to treat the strip club like a real club. She wasn't her to just socialize. As a matter of fact, she wasn't socializing with anyone who wasn't spending money. She had a goal to attain: three lap dances per hour. To make her goal fun, she and Dee-Dee had a personal bet to see who could get the most lap dances by the end of the night.

"I think I got one?" Shantell remarked.

Dee-Dee replied, "Do your thing."

Shantell had spotted her target from across the room. He was an older black gentleman who sat at the bar, nursing a drink. From behind she approached the man undetected. She wasn't quite sure of how she was going to break the ice but Shantell knew she would figure that out as she went along.

"You mind if I sit here and rest my feet for a minute?" Shantell whispered. "I'm not used to these heels."

"No, go right ahead," the man replied. "What's yo' name, sweetheart? I ain't never seen you before."

The man recklessly eyeballed Shantell, taking inventory of her body. There was no doubt he liked what he saw.

"My name is So Sexy," Shantell told him. "What's yours?"

"My name is Jason," he said. "You sure got the right name. It fits you to a tee."

"Thanks!"

"Can I get you something?" Want some Alize or shot of Hennessy?"

"Nah, I don't drink," she admitted. "But I do take donations."

The guy laughed at her terminology for a tip. He thought it was cute. Most of all, he thought she was cute. He complied with her request, sliding her a five-dollar bill.

Shantell's easygoing demeanor and bright smile seemed to invite conversation from the man. He began spilling his guts out. He told her everything from his martial status to his job title. Shantell pretended to be impressed by what he was saying. After all, this was a fantasy world and Shantell was in the business of selling dreams.

It was obvious that he was in the market to buy a dream, from the way he kept showering Shantell with bills and attention. She had a subtle approach that seemed to suggest she was genuinely interested in him. But that couldn't have been further from the truth. If Shantell saw this guy outside the club, she wouldn't give him the time of day.

Shantell wound up sitting with the man for damn near an hour. When his money was gone, so was she.

"Well, Jason, it's been nice talking to you. But now I gotta get back to work."

Shantell gave the man the impression that sitting with him wasn't work at all. The guy was flattered that she enjoyed his conversation. She left the man on a good note: as a satisfied customer.

Not to be outdone, Dee-Dee worked the club, getting several lap dances from every man who loved her big ass. For this being their first night, the duo was doing great. They were beautiful with great bodies and extremely friendly. This was a profitable combination.

Shantell had more enthusiasm and energy. She was not only chasing money. Shantell was chasing a dream: to get out of the projects. This led her to embrace her environment and maximize each moment at the club. Every man she laid her eyes on represented a dollar sign.

As the night wore on, the club began to fill up with strippers and customers. There was fierce competition for a dollar. The girls rose to the occasion, becoming more aggressive.

They stepped their game up and went after a dollar with a vengeance. Their acts would get them into their first confrontation.

In a dimly lit area of the club, Shantell furiously grinded her hips against a customer's private parts. She could feel his erection poking through his denim jeans. Shantell knew he was enjoying this lap dance by the way he acted. His hands were everywhere. He gripped her ass from time to time and spoke real dirty to her.

"Damn, Shorty, what you doing tonight?" he whispered. "I wanna fuck da shit outta you, for real. My pipe game is tight."

Shantell never said a word in response. She merely smiled and kept making eye contact. She busied herself lap dancing, working him into a sexual frenzy.

"You sexy as hell! Shorty, what's good? Can we make this a private party?"

From out of nowhere, a stripper rapidly approached from Shantell's blind side. If the mean mug that was plastered on her face was any indication of how she felt, then she wasn't happy.

"What the fuck you think you doing?" Passion yelled. "Get off of him!"

Grabbing Shantell's arm, Passion snatched her up off the man. If looks could kill, then Shantell and the man would be dead. What Shantell did not know was that the man she had given the lap dance to was Passion's baby's father.

Oh, nigger, you got money for a lap dance but you can't take care of yo' daughter." Passion announced. "You a worthless piece of shit! A deadbeat fucking dad."

Shantell didn't have anything to do with this, yet she had everything to do with it. She felt that Passion had violated her by touching her. The thought of it infuriated Shantell. While Passion focused her attention on the man, Shantell shoved the girl with all her might, knocking her to the floor.

By this time the man got up and stood between both combatants. He extended his arms to keep them separate. A shouting match ensued. Passion's friends came to her aid and Dee-Dee came to Shantell's side. Together they braced for whatever trouble that might come.

Security guards from all over rushed in to break up the potential melee. All parties involved were separated and the man was removed from the club. After a while, things calmed down and the club returned to normal. Finally Dee-Dee and Shantell were able to talk.

"What happened?" Dee-Dee inquired.

"Nothing really," Shantell replied. "That bitch got mad 'cause I was dancing with her baby daddy! She grabbed me, so I pushed her back."

"Okay. I didn't know what happened. I saw them roll up on you, so I came over to help," Dee-Dee stated. "If I'm around, I ain't gonna let nothing happen to you."

Shantell was touched by the statement. She was glad that Dee-Dee had held her down like that. After all, she hardly knew Shantell. For that act, Shantell would be forever loyal to her. In a moment of drama Dee-Dee had left a good lasting impression.

For the rest of the night, Dee-Dee and Shantell barely left each other's sight. They were inseparable. If one fought, then they both were going to fight. From then on, that's the way it was going to be.

Finally it was time for Club Champagne to close. Shantell and Dee-Dee expected trouble but none came their way. The other strippers must have done a background check on them. Though Charlotte was a big city, it still retained that small-town feel. Here, everybody knew everybody.

Once the strippers found out who she was and more importantly, where Shantell was from, they didn't mess with her. Suddenly they had a newfound respect for her. She came from the projects, Piedmont Courts, a place of struggle. They figured she had to be wild and she wasn't the one to fuck with, at least not if they didn't want to suffer the consequences.

Before the club emptied out, Shantell and Dee-Dee exited with a mixture of strippers and customers. Both the strippers and customers actively solicited sexual favors for money. Even Shantell was approached by an ultra-aggressive patron.

"What's up, Shawty?" he asked. "I'm trying to do a few things. What's good with you? I'm saying, what a li'l head gonna cost me?"

The average chick might have been offended by this statement. Shantell wasn't the average chick or the average stripper, for that matter. The name of the game for her was survival. Shantell's main objective was clear: she was here to make money. She wasn't passing up a dollar.

Without a moment's hesitation, Shantell accepted the man's invitation, then they negotiated a price for some oral sex. When that was done, they went back to his car to commit the act.

After the money was exchanged, Shantell got into the car and immediately grabbed the man's crotch, just to see what he was working with. Judging from the handful of dick she gripped, the man was holding. Shantell began stroking the man's dick until it was fully erect.

"Lean back," she commanded. "Relax."

Shantell ripped open his zipper and reached inside to produce his penis. Instantly, she went down on the man. Shantell began to tease him, licking the head of his dick with the tip of her tongue. The man began to moan with pleasure; the noises he emitted only made Shantell work harder to please him. She began to take the man deeper and deeper into her mouth till his dick was touching the back of her throat. Now his dick was completely coated with saliva.

Shantell looked up at the guy, making eye contact as she sucked his dick. This turned the guy on even more.

"Yeah, suck that dick, bitch," he spat. "That shit feels so fucking good!"

Just the sight of a chick so fine sucking his dick, damn near bought him to a climax. He continued to watch as Shantell ran circles around his dick with her tongue.

Suddenly Shantell brought her hands into play. She began to jerk him off and suck him off simultaneously. This really seemed to do the trick.

"Damn girl, I'm about to cum."

Shantell pulled her face away from the man's dick. For the man to cum in her mouth would cost him extra. If he didn't know it, he soon would.

"Damn why you stop?" he questioned. "I was just about to bust a nut."

"You can't cum in my mouth for free," Shantell stated. "You gotta pay extra for that."

The man reached into his pocket and tossed Shantell a twenty-dollar bill. That seemed to bridge the communication gap, and Shantell went back to business. She brought the man right back to the point of pleasure he had experienced previously; only this time, she didn't stop. In no time the man began to climax. Shantell continued to suck his dick with a vengeance as he came in her mouth.

When the man was done, Shantell opened the car door and spit a glob of semen onto the ground. Then she walked off as nothing ever happened. It was all in a day's work.

From a safe distance, Dee-Dee watched her friend's back. Initially she thought that it was a bad idea. Dee-Dee was cautious without coming across as scared. Still, she didn't judge Shantell on her act. She knew her situation. Shantell had to do what she had to do. Dee-Dee just wasn't ready to put herself out there like that.

That night, both Shantell and Dee-Dee would get a glimpse of their collective futures, money and men.

Chapter 4

It ain't all good

On her day off Shantell decided to take her daughter Jordan to the park.

"Peek-a-boo, I see you," Shantell said.

"Pee-boo," Jordan said in baby talk. "c u."

Jordan was a bright kid, who caught on quick. Patty-cake and Peek-a-boo were two of her favorite games. She loved playing rhyming and sing a long games with her mother. Shantell could relate easily to her daughter because she was a kid at heart. Anyone who was lucky enough to view moments like these could tell that these two shared an intense bond.

"Boo!" Shantell yelled.

In reaction to her mother's playfulness, Jordan tried to hide her face behind her small hands. But she didn't do a very good job. Shantell gazed into her daughter's eye lovingly. She tried to time her, so she would catch her with her face exposed. But as she stared at Jordan, she forgot that they were even playing a game.

Jordan beat her to the punch.

"Pee-boo. I see u mommy!" She exclaimed happily. "I vin."

Shantell broke out into a toothy smile as her daughter ran up to her and hugged her. Shantell bent down and picked her up, placing Jordan on the bench.

Sitting side by side, Shantell and her daughter bore a striking resemblance. That fact warmed Shantell's heart. Jordan was her everything, her reason for being. A feeling of completeness washed over her. She didn't look at her child as a burden; instead she viewed Jordan as a blessing. In a life full of horrible wrongs, Jordan was the lone bright spot.

"Play Patty cake mommy." Jordan playful screamed.

"Patty cake, Patty cake," Shantell chimed. "Make a cake, put in da oven and watch it bake..."

Shantell lived vicariously through he daughter. She re-lived her days of youth and innocence, which were gone. She vowed to keep her daughter carefree. She wanted Jordan to be a child for a long as possible. If she did her job as a parent well then she would insulate her daughter from the street life. And shelter her from all harm.

At Three years old Jordan's mind was sharp as a whip. She played right along with her mother. Through constant repetition, Jordan picked up the nursery rhymes.

Suddenly in the middle of the game, Jordan stopped and pointed to something.

"Mommy. Swing. Swing," She suddenly said. "C'mon!"

Soon as the words were out her mouth, she took off running, as fast as her little legs would carry her. Shantell was right behind her, in hot pursuit. Sounds of loud laughter and giggles filled the air. Though the park was packed to capacity, with parents and children, trying to catch one of the last few warm days, one would have thought this was their own private little play ground. Shantell and Jordan were in their own world. They showed no interest in socializing with anyone else but each other.

"Wee, mommy!" Jordan called out.

Shantell watched over and over again, as her child slide down the giant blue slide. It seemed like Jordan was really enjoy herself."

"Ooooh, look at you." Shantell commented. "You such a big girl, Jordan."

One good thing that came out of being a teenage mother was, Shantell was able to physically play with her daughter for countless hours at time. These were her child's formative years,

Shantell was sure she would remember this later in life. She was laying the groundwork for a bond that would last a lifetime.

As afternoon turned to evening, the park began to thin out. Thus bringing and end to their fun filled day. Shantell and Jordan relaxed on the park bench taking in the sights and sounds. While sitting on the park bench, a pair of joggers slowly came into view.

"C'mon ma," The woman yelled. "One more lap."

As they passed, Shantell stared at the woman and her daughter enviously. Seeing mother and daughter together triggered something in her. Suddenly she began to wonder about her own mother. She wondered exactly what she was up to. It had been months since they had last seen each other. Now Shantell felt it was time to seek her mother out.

On any given day the feelings Shantell had for her mother fluctuated. Sometimes she hated her and sometimes she loved her dearly. Shantell was on an emotional roller coast.

◈

Shantell arrived at her apartment complex just as dusk had settled over the city of Charlotte. After parking her car, she walked towards her apartment, with Jordan in tow. Opening the door, she found her housemate Dee-Dee, in the kitchen frying some chicken for dinner.

"Hey, Jay!" Dee-Dee happily hollered.

Jordan ran over to Dee-Dee and affectionately hugged her leg. In response Dee-Dee bent over and picked her up. She was as excited to see the baby, as Jordan was to see her.

Shantell couldn't help but be touched by this scene. This was one of the many reasons she loved Dee-Dee so much. Dee-Dee showed Jordan so much love and affection. How couldn't she love her?

"Damn, it smells good in here." Shantell stated. "Girl, what else you cookin' besides that chicken?"

Shantell could see a few other pots on the stove. Since the aroma from the chicken was so strong, it overrode the other scents.

Dee-Dee replied, "I got some yellow rice, collard greens, and Mac and cheese. And some grape kool-aid in the frig."

"Damn. That sound good.' Shantell thought to herself.

"Dee could you fix Jordan sumthin' ta eat?" She asked. "I gotta go somewhere?"

"Where you off too?" Dee-Dee inquired. "Why don't you wait a minute, dinner is almost ready. What's so important?"

"I'm gonna go see 'bout my mother." She announced. "I gotta funny feeling."

Dee-Dee was well aware of Shantell and her mother's volatile relationship. One night Shantell had broke down and told her everything. Shantell and Dee-Dee had talked deeply about their personal struggles. Shantell had made her ill feelings for her mother no secret. Now Dee-Dee wondered what bought about the sudden change. Still she felt it wasn't her place to question it.

"Alright." Dee-Dee said. "Be careful."

Shantell exited the apartment knowing her daughter was in good hands. She got into her car and jumped on highway 77 headed towards her old stomping grounds, Piedmont courts. .

Arriving at the projects, Shantell quickly noticed nothing had changed. The same drug dealers were out pedaling their wares. Basically the same people who were messed up when she left, almost a year ago, were still messed up. The more things had changed the more they had stayed the same. It was almost like to make it in life one had to leave the hood. But some people refused to, they were born in the projects, their children were born in the projects and possibly their children's children would be. .

Navigating her way through the concrete jungle, Shantell saw a few familiar faces, she stopped and said her hello's and went about her business. She didn't give anybody much time to get in her business. She wasn't there for that.

Approaching her mother's apartment, she suddenly began to have second thoughts. 'Why am I here?' She mused. 'I should just turn back around and go home. Ain't nuttin' for me here no more.'

Quickly, Shantell pushed all those negative thoughts from her mind. She came to her senses. In her heart she knew, that regardless of what transpired in that house, that woman whom she had little or no respect for was still her mother. She was family and she couldn't disown her so easily. They had a history together, good or bad it couldn't be erased from her memory.

Shantell reached the back door, knocked loudly twice and waited for someone to answer the door. Then she did it again. From the outside, she could clearly hear people scrambling around inside. Soon she heard the sounds of footsteps coming towards the door.

"Wwwhhhooo!" Someone yelled. "Who da fuck knockin' on da door like they the police?"

A puzzled expression spread across Shantell's face. She wondered who was inside her mother's house and exactly what were they doing there.

Without a moment's hesitation, the door flew open. Shantell stood face to face with a pint-sized drug dealer. One look at him and she knew what was going on. Her former home had been turned into a full fledged crack house.

The kid didn't recognize Shantell, he thought she was a customer in search of some product. One thing he knew about drug users they came in all sizes shapes and colors. So he didn't question her appearance at the back door. As a matter of fact, he hoped she was indeed a smoker, as good as she looked, he planned on turning a trick with her.

"What's up? How many you want?" He asked.

At that point Shantell lost it. She couldn't believe this young kid was treating her like a fiend in her own house.

"What?!" She yelled. "Motherfucker I don't do drugs. So take ya little rocks and shove 'em up ya ass. Now, where the hell is my mother Brenda?"

It was then that the money hungry kid knew he made a serious mistake.

While he stood in the door way looking defiantly at Shantell, she suddenly pushed passed him. Entering her mother's house she was about to see, first hand, how her living conditions went from bad to worst.

"Ma." She called out.

"She ain't here." The youngster answered.

"Where da fuck she at? Huh?" She screamed.

Rather than deal with Shantell's nasty attitude the young dealer fled the house. He decided to come back when she was gone.

The farther Shantell walked into the house the more disgusted she became. Rodents could be seen darting around the kitchen. Garbage overflowed in the trash can causing. A foul odor . All her mother's living room furniture was gone, replaced by a bunch of milk crates. The apartment was so empty her voice echoed off the walls.

Suddenly two crackheads, a man and a woman, scurried down the stairs; they smelled just as bad as they looked.

"Hi." They seemed to say in unison.

Shantell just shot them the evil eye; her look conveyed exactly how she felt. The blood in her veins was boiling, she felt like hurting somebody. Then she realized that her anger was misappropriated at the wrong people. They only did what her drug addicted mother allowed them to do.

Continuing, on her search through the apartment, she climbed up the stairs. There Shantell discovered it was the same story. Everything of value had been sold to feed her mother's addiction. Her bedroom set was long gone; the only thing her mother had to sleep on was an air mattress. Nature called so she headed towards the bathroom. Shantell walked into the bathroom and was greeted by a toilet bowl full of feces. The stench was unbearable, she quickly retreated. Suddenly she realized she didn't have to use the bathroom so badly after all.

Unable to find her mother at home, Shantell canvassed the neighborhood, going door to door, of all the known drug houses. She even knocked on few neighbors doors that she knew.

"Stand out there long enough and you'll see her." The elderly lady suggested.

Shantell did just that, she waited and waited till her mother appeared. Out of nowhere she spotted two frail looking women coming directly towards her. Shantell stared hard at them till, she was sure that the smaller woman was indeed her mother, Brenda. And the women had just copped some drugs and weren't about to let each other out of their eyesight till they got what was due to them. Neither trusted the other as far as they could throw her.

"...Damn, the boys sure did bless us. You see the size of that rock. It was fat." One woman announced.

"Us? They blessed me! They wouldn't have even served you." Brenda countered. "You burnt them boys so many times..... I'm given' you ya five dollars worth and that's it...."

The woman interrupted, "If it wasn't fa me you couldn't even got a twenty."

"So." Brenda flatly stated. "Anyway you, still owe me from that hit you bummed off me last week. Yeah, remember that?"

Back and forth the two crack fiends bickered over who should get the bigger percentage of the drug. Distracted by the argument they never once noticed Shantell standing in the yard.

"Ma!" She cried out.

The voice had caught them both off guard. Brenda and her junkie friend both looked in Shantell's direction, since they both had children. But even in her drug induced haze, Brenda knew that voice from anywhere. She knew that this shadowy figure was a child of hers.

"Shantell?" She responded. "Is that you?"

Shantell walked over to her mother. Even in the darkness she could see that her mother was looking bad. To her Brenda looked like death in the face, her jaws were sunken in and her eyes seemed to bulge out of the socket. She was so boney, her over coat was bigger than her. Her body looked like it was wasting away.

Even in this condition Shantell felt like her mother would at least greet her, with a hug. After all she hadn't seen her in almost a year. But it wasn't to be, Brenda stood there emotionless, as if she saw her daughter everyday. Shantell was crushed, 'Where was the love?" She wondered. After all it was love that brought her to Brenda's door despite everything.

Shantell felt that if her mother wasn't woman enough to show her some emotion, then she would be the bigger person in this situation. She reached out and pulled her mother, and held her tight as if her life depended on it.

Though Shantell was a young woman, in terms of her age, inside she still was a kid who needed her mother. And this was her way of showing it. Through something so simple yet affectionate as an embrace. Just to be in her mother's arms meant the world to her. Brenda just didn't know. Or maybe she was too high to even care.

"Excuse us!" Shantell barked. "Can you give us some privacy please?"

It took every bit of restraint for Shantell not to get ignorant with the stranger. She reminded herself she wasn't here for that. She was just here to see her mother, nothing more.

Shantell continued, "How you doin' Ma? How's everything?"

"Oh, I'm ok." Brenda pretended. "How's everything with you and the baby?"

"We're alright." She stated. "Ya grand daughter getting' big."

"I'll bet." Brenda fired back. "Jordan always had a healthy appetite."

This basic conversation was a start for the two women. When Shantell had lived in the house, she had gone for weeks without even speaking to her mother. There were so many things she wanted to say to her, but she decided against it. That would only open up old wounds that still were in the process of healing. Besides that this visit wasn't about her, it was about Brenda. Shantell couldn't bring herself to be selfish at a time like this.

Sure She could have chastised her mother for her living conditions or for her choice of lifestyle for that matter. But she didn't. She pretended as if none of the events had transpired and she didn't see her mother in her current state of despair. Though Shantell had the upper hand now, she decided not to treat Brenda less than a woman, less than her mother.

"Dis ain't you Ma. When you gonna get off dat stuff ?" Shantell begged. "You can't go on like dis forever you know? I'm scared for you. It's dangerous out here."

"Baby, I'ma go to rehab soon. I'm getting' sick and tired of this shit myself. Believe me."

Shantell looked her mother dead in the eye and saw no truth to what she was saying. Most of all she heard no signs of sincerity in her voice. To her without those two things her words were meaningless. Brenda was lying to herself because she sure wasn't fooling Shantell.

Out the corner of her eye, Shantell could see her mother's associate growing more and more impatient. She kept fidgeting around in her pockets, as if she was looking for something. Even her mother looked like she was ready to go, her eyes darted around the yard.

"Look Ma, I ain't gonna hold you up any longer. I see y'all ready to go do whatever. But listen here go my cell number. When you get ya'self together give me a call." Shantell told her.

"Alright, I will." Brenda swore. "You'll be the first person I call. I promise baby."

With that Shantell walked off, comfortable in knowing that she did her part. Shantell extended a help hand to her mother. There was nothing more she could do but wait. The ball was in Brenda's court it was up to her to make the next move.

Behind her Shantell heard the back door open and slam shut. She knew damn well that her mother was up to no good but she was powerless to stop her. Brenda was a grown woman, she had no authority over her. To Shantell Brenda was like a drowning person, if She tried to save her now, Brenda would bring them both down. And Shantell wasn't about to allow that. She had her daughter Jordan to think about. Nothing came before her, not even her own mother.

The days turned into weeks, and weeks turned into months without any call from Brenda. So Shantell pushed her mother out of her mind. Once again, she felt stupid for even extending and invitation to her...Brenda would never get off drugs. Shantell felt like her mother would meet her maker while getting high. Or she would die in some drug related incident, shot down like a dog in the street by some young drug dealer. Shantell feared that one of these two fates would befall her mother She was doing anything and everything to get high.

When Shantell did get the news she wasn't the least bit surprised. Though it hadn't happened like she thought, Brenda was arrested in a house raid. The police had kicked in her door due to the high level of drug traffic. Besides Brenda, a few drug dealers and crack fiends were arrested.

Shantell hoped that her arrest would be a blessing in disguise. She hoped that this brush with the law would scare Brenda straight, that her time in the Mecklenburg county jail would get her clean. She hoped that jail would save her mother's life as it had done countless others in the hood.

While her mother was in jail the only thing that Shantell could do, was to pray. She prayed that god would lift the curse, known as crack from her mother's soul. She prayed that one day they could be a family again.

❧❧

A few months later...

When Shantell got the word, she didn't believe it was true. She had heard the whispers for years now. Still she paid them no mind. She knew how people gossiped. So she chalked it up as that a rumor or just idle talk. This was until she began seeing reports of it on the news. It had taken her some time but Shantell eventually gotten around to investigating it herself. Now, here she was parked on the side of the road, with her daughter in tow, staring in disbelief.

If seeing is believing, then her eyes were bearing witness right now. Currently her vision was testifying to the finality of Piedmont Courts. This was the end of her childhood existence as she knew it.

"Well I'll be damned!" She cursed. "Look at this shit here. They really are tearing this rotten bitch down."

There it was dozens of two story brick, dilapidated buildings huddled close together with no signs of life. Piedmont Courts, the place she was raised, was abandoned, boarded up, fenced off and scheduled to be demolished by the city of Charlotte,. The place looked like a ghost town, even in its heyday Piedmont Courts was a graveyard for lost souls.

Dancing at Club Champagne had literally been the best thing that ever happened to Shantell, at least financially. Each and every day she proved she could not only survive, but thrive in a game with grown women five to ten years her senior. With the money she made dancing, Shantell was able to improve the living conditions of not only herself but her baby as well.. In six months she was able to stack enough paper to finally move out of Piedmont Courts.

Therefore she didn't bear witness to the mass exodus of people from Piedmont Courts over the course of a few months. She thought it would always be around forever, to ruin generation after generation of young lives.

As Shantell sat in her car staring at the abandoned buildings her memories came alive. She could vividly see all the single black mothers, the fatherless children, the drug dealers, the drug addicts and prostitutes. She could see countless people being engulfed by negativity.

Shantell reflected on the adult like situations she was placed in at a young age. Suddenly she realized she never had a chance to be young.

Dozens of memories flashed across her mind. Shantell became angry. She began to cry. Her brother had taken more from her than she ever imaged.

For awhile, relocating had seemed to rejuvenate Shantell. When Shantell changed addresses she effectively changed her fortunes.

Her life in the projects seemed so long ago, but still Shantell hadn't forgotten just what transpired there. But in a few days,

Piedmonts Courts would be a distant memory. The projects would be gone but her scars wouldn't fade away so easily.

This reunion had been imminent. For Shantell there would be no sorrow in parting, there were no memorable moments for her to cherish. She put her car in gear and slowly pulled off. In the back of her mind she knew even with the destruction of Piedmont Courts that wasn't enough to put an end to her questionable past.

❧❧

From the outside of the apartment, Shantell could hear Dee-Dee raising her voice in harsh tones. She was cursing somebody out over the phone. This surprised her because it wasn't even Dee-Dee's style. Dee-Dee didn't speak in the same vernacular as other females, so when she did get ghetto, her words carried more weight.

"Look, motherfucker stop calling' me! I told you a thousand times I don't wanna be bothered. It's over! What part of that don't you understand?" she shouted. "You need to build a bridge over it and move on."

Upon hearing that, Shantell automatically knew who Dee-Dee was talking to,: her ex-boyfriend, Mario. Ever since the two women had moved in together he had steadily become a problem. Mario didn't take rejection easily. He was persistent with his bullshit; he went from harassing Dee-Dee on the phone to even showing up at the club from time to time. Personally, Shantell was beginning to have bad vibes about the whole situation.

More and more these types of heated exchanges were becoming commonplace. At first Dee-Dee tried to hide her verbal disputes, but Shantell would catch her in the bathroom having secret conversations in hushed tones.

Shantell had told Dee-Dee over and over again to be careful. She warned her not to argue with Mario. She wished Dee-Dee would not even accept his phone calls; she saw no sense in it. Shantell thought that talking to him would only encourage him to keep doing what he was doing. Too bad Dee-Dee didn't see it that way.

Mario was Dee-Dee's first love, so there was some sort of bond or history that the two shared. Since Shantell had never been in love, it was impossible for her to understand it. Any explanation she came up with wasn't good enough.

"Well, if you wanted to be with me so bad, you should have thought about that before you got that hoe pregnant," Dee-Dee scolded. "What I told you? You have a baby with somebody else and it's over... You did it to yo'self, Mario. You ain't got nobody to blame except you!"

Dee-Dee sat speechless on the phone, listening to Mario cop a plea. He apologized over and over again. He even denied being the baby's father. Still, Dee-Dee didn't believe one word. Mario's words fell on deaf ears. Dee-Dee was so engrossed in her conversation she never even heard Shantell enter the apartment. Shantell entered the living room, carrying her sleeping daughter in her arms, shaking her head. Dee-Dee returned her friend's disapproving look with a smile.

Shantell thought that Dee-Dee was playing a potentially dangerous game. She felt that her friend was sending Mario the wrong message. Shantell had voiced her opinion once before to Dee-Dee, which her friend didn't take too well. After that, Shantell promised herself never to do it again. Who was she to tell Dee-Dee about her safety? Dee -Dee was her own woman. As long as Mario didn't bring that mess around here, there was nothing more Shantell could say or do.

"Better leave that nigger the fuck alone," Shantell commented.

Dee-Dee put one finger to her lip, giving Shantell the quiet sign.

"Look I gotta go," Dee-Dee spoke into the phone. "Why? None of ya business! You not my man! I said I gotta go. Bye!"

Upon hanging up the phone Dee-Dee threw her hands in the air out of frustration. She was confused. She didn't know whether or not she was going to break away completely from Mario, or give him one more chance. But if the truth be told, Dee-Dee wasn't in love with Mario. She feared him. She thought Mario was crazy.

"What's up, girl?" Dee-Dee said. "That was Mario on the phone, stressing me the hell out, again!"

"Anyway!" Shantell spat. "I don't even wanna hear it. That's your business."

"Whatever!" Dee-Dee joked. "Anyway, where was y'all all morning? I woke up and you and the baby were gone."

"Me and Jordan took a little ride. We cruised around town. I just wanted get some fresh air."

"I hear that," Dee-Dee expressed. "I can't wait till I have a kid, so I can do little fun stuff like that."

"Don't rush yourself, girlfriend. It ain't all that it cracked up to be." Don't get me wrong, I love my daughter, but sometimes I need a break or a day off. But ain't no breaks in this motherhood thing. It's every day, all day."

Shantell and Dee-Dee had become very close since their initial meeting. This was evident by their current living arrangement. Shantell was a loner by nature, so for her to allow Dee-Dee to become her roommate spoke volumes about her feelings for her.

Dee-Dee's presence in the apartment seemed to have a settling effect on both Shantell and Jordan. Not only did she help out with the rent and household chores, but also helped ease Shantell's motherly responsibilities. Dee-Dee would get up and feed or watch the baby whenever Shantell didn't feel like it or was too tired to. Dee-Dee showed Jordan so much love that Shantell couldn't help but love her back. In the ultimate act that cemented their friendship, Shantell named Dee-Dee as the baby's godmother. God forbid, if something happened to her, she knew that Dee-Dee was more than capable of loving and caring for her daughter.

Dee-Dee was also good to have around for another reason. She was Shantell's alter ego, her conscience. She wasn't as brash or daring when it came to making money at the strip club. Shantell had a real hardcore attitude in areas where Dee-Dee was hesitant or unsure. Shantell went all out for that bread. A lot of times Dee-Dee would intervene when she saw that Shantell was out of control. She was always that calming influence that could bring Shantell back to her senses.

It was too bad that Dee-Dee didn't exercise the same restraint in her own personal life.

❧❧❧

It was another typical night at Club Champagne. Shantell and Dee-Dee were on the job. As always, they were chasing the almighty dollar, hustling hard for that money. Dee-Dee was doing her required dance sets up on the stage when she suddenly bolted from the stage. Shantell had seen her walk off the stage before her set was completed and followed her. They headed straight for the locker room.

Dee-Dee wore a frustrated look on her face. She lit up a cigarette to calm her nerves.

"I don't believe this shit," Dee-Dee spat. "This shit is going too far."

"What's wrong?" Shantell asked. "Why you leave the stage like that?"

"Girl, you ain't gonna believe this shit. I saw that nigger Mario standing there, staring at me from the bar. He had a funny look on his face and it kinda fucked me up."

Dee-Dee took long drags from her cigarette. She exhaled huge clouds of smoke. Momentarily it seemed to calm her nerves. Shantell had never seen her friend so shook up like this. She saw something strange in Dee-Dee's eyes, and it was fear.

"That's it! I'm going to go back out there and tell that nigger off," Shantell ranted. "This nigger is going too far. First the phone calls, now this. I mean, what's next? Describe that nigger to me. What he got on?"

Dee-Dee replied, "He tall and light -skinned. He got on a red New York fitted baseball cap and a red-and-white Snow-man shirt. You can't miss him."

As Shantell left the locker room, Dee-Dee didn't even put up a protest. Now she was just beginning to see that Mario was much more than a thorn in her side. He was a problem. Maybe, just maybe, she needed someone to intervene. She hoped Shantell could run him away. Maybe she could talk some sense into him, explain to him that Dee-Dee didn't want him any more.

Where is this nigger at? Shantell mused as she walked around the club.

Every possible place that a patron could possibly be in the club, Shantell looked. She looked by the bar, by the pool table area, upstairs in the champagne and the VIP rooms. She couldn't find anybody who came close to fitting that description. Finally, Shantell asked around and she was told a guy matching that description had left already.

"I looked but I couldn't find that nigger nowhere. Somebody said he left right after we walked into the locker room," Shantell admitted.

It seemed like a burden had been lifted off her chest. Dee-Dee's mood immediately began to change. She began to make lighthearted jokes at her predicament.

"I guess I gotta be more careful who I give this pussy to, huh? Just my luck I wound up with a fucking psychopathic, stalking-ass nigger!"

"You need to take out a restraining order on his ass," Shantell told her. "Something is seriously wrong wit' that nigger."

Dee-Dee went on to explain to Shantell how she didn't want to involve the police in this matter. How she still had some feelings for Mario and she didn't want to see him possibly arrested. At one point in time he had been very good to her, so she felt she owed him that. Dee-Dee said she would call his mother and explained the situation to her. She felt that Mario would listen to his mother.

After they talked it out, Dee-Dee and Shantell headed back into the club. Shantell picked up where she had left off, chasing that paper. She had immediately put Mario out of her mind. For Dee-Dee, it was a lot harder for her to get her mind right. Mario's presence haunted her long after he had disappeared.

కి౪ఞ

Meanwhile, outside in the parking lot, Mario sat inside his car, fuming. The sight of his lady, Dee-Dee, dancing naked for other men in the club had enraged him. It took everything in his power to refrain from jumping up on the stage and pulling her off it. Mario may have been crazy but he was far from stupid. He knew that an act like that might spark more trouble than he could handle by himself. So rather than to continue to spy on Dee-Dee, he left under his own power.

Suddenly Mario reached into his glove compartment and grabbed a pen and piece of paper. He began to feverishly jolt down his thoughts and feelings, some of which weren't comprehensible to anyone but him.

"Dee-Dee, when I saw you up on that stage it hurt me to my heart," the note began. *"I know I made mistakes, but so did you. You said some mean things but I forgive you. Nobody could love you like I will. I know you still feel me. They say if you love something let it go, but I can't. I'll love you to death."*

◈◈◈

After tipping out Shantell and Dee-Dee left Club Champagne. They headed to their car, totally exhausted. They both seemed to spot the note attached to the windshield at the same time. At first they thought it was a party flyer but upon further inspection they knew what it was. Since Shantell was the first to reach the car, she picked up the note and read it to herself.

Shantell read every word of Mario's note. His chilling words disturbed her. When she was finished, she passed the note to Dee-Dee. Dee-Dee's hands began to tremble as she read along. By the time she was through reading, she was a nervous wreck. She couldn't think straight.

"Mario's just hurt, that's all," she explained. "He doesn't really mean it. That's just talk."

At first, Dee-Dee tried to downplay the note's deadly undertones. She made all kinds of weak excuse for her ex-boyfriend.

The fear on Dee-Dee's face was evident. To Shantell, her mouth was saying one thing but her body was saying something totally different.

"So this nigger loves you? Huh?" Shantell asked. "If he does, he got a funny way of showing it."

Shantell hated to be sarcastic at a time like this, but right about now she would do anything to get her point across. She really believed Mario was dangerous. If only she could convince Dee-Dee.

Right there in the parking lot, the two women had a lengthy conversation about Mario. Dee-Dee began recounting the events that led to their break up. She told Shantell about his cheating ways, including the other woman Mario had gotten pregnant. She told her about the arguments, then the physical abuse. Dee-Dee admitted that he had even given her a black eye and broke her arm at one time or another. It didn't take long for Dee-Dee to paint a picture of domestic abuse. Shantell came to the conclusion that Mario was indeed over possessive.

Distraught, Dee-Dee handed her keys over to Shantell so she could drive. After piling into the car they took off, heading home. Shantell pulled out of the parking lot and for the rest of the way home, the duo drove in silence.

Unbeknownst to them, as soon as they merged into traffic, another car had begun to follow them from a safe distance.

CHAPTER 5
LOVE YA TA DEATH

After a good night's sleep, Dee-Dee awoke with the same problem on her mind: Mario. Although she had every right to go to the authorities and seek some type of police action against him, like a restraining order or an order of protection, she chose to take a diplomatic approach. She called Mario's mother.

"Good morning, Mrs. Hughes." Dee-Dee affectionately said. "It's me, Denise."

"Oh, baby. Sorry I couldn't make out your voice. I haven't heard from you in so long," Mrs. Hughes replied. "You can keep in touch, you know."

"Yes, I know, ma'am. Lately, I've been a little busy. I apologize for that. Please forgive me," Dee-Dee pleaded. "I won't let it happen again."

Dee-Dee had the utmost respect for Mrs. Hughes. She looked at her as a surrogate mother of sorts. She had a special place in her heart for Mrs. Hughes ever since she had let Dee-Dee live there, rent free, for a few years. Mrs. Hughes had taken Dee-Dee in after her own mother had thrown her out. She let her move in, no questions asked. For that, Dee-Dee was indebted forever to her.

Dee-Dee continued. "Anyway, the reason I called is… it's about Mario. As you know, me and him are no longer together. And…for whatever reason, Mario keeps bothering me. I don't wanna be bothered with him no more, but he's not listen to me. I was hoping you could talk to him for me."

"Oh, baby I wish you kids would stop that nonsense and get back together," Mrs. Hughes insisted. "God knows ya'll love each other."

Needless to say, this was not the type of reply that Dee-Dee expected from her. Then again, what did she expect? Mrs. Hughes was older than your average parent. She had Mario very late in life. As result, she had been a lot more lenient on Mario than her other children. He, in turn, took advantage of his mother's kindness from childhood to adulthood. Mrs. Hughes had a childlike perception of her son; in her eyes, he could do no wrong. No matter what her son did, she sided with him.

Dee-Dee decided to spare Mrs. Hughes the details. She couldn't bring herself to tell Mario's mother exactly what he was doing or what he had done to her. Besides, she wouldn't believe it, anyway.

"No, Mrs. Hughes, I don't think we'll be getting back together anytime soon. Our relationship is finished."

"Denise, you shouldn't talk like that. You never know, so don't be like that. You kids need to just sit down face to face and talk it out. That's the key to everything. Nowadays, y'all kids don't communicate. Y'all just make rush decisions, and that's not good."

"But..." Dee-Dee began. "Forget it Mrs. Hughes. Nice speaking to you. I'll be in touch real soon. Goodbye."

"Okay, baby. You do that. Think about what I said in the meantime. You know haste makes waste. Y'all belong together."

Dee-Dee didn't get anywhere by talking to Mrs. Hughes. As a matter of fact, she came away more frustrated than ever. She couldn't believe how naïve Mario's mother was. She was blind to the overly aggressive ways of her son. If ignorance was bliss, then she was in heaven. They didn't make women like her anymore.

From the comforts of her bedroom, Shantell had over-heard Dee-Dee's secret conversation. Judging from the side of the conversation she had heard, her friend was no closer to the resolution of this problem than the day it began. Shantell got up to have another talk with Dee-Dee.

"Who was that you were talking to?" Shantell asked.

"Mario's mom." Dee-Dee replied flatly.

"Well, what she have to say?"

"She didn't say a damn thing. Mario got her brain-washed. I don't know why I even called her. That lady is stuck on stupid," Dee-Dee insisted. "I ain't never seen no shit like that in my life."

Shantell fired back, "Well, I guess you ain't got no choice but to go to the police, then, since your way didn't work. Whether you know it or not, you're not the only one involved in this. You got me and my baby involved too. Think about us. What about our safety?"

The statement hit home. Dee-Dee began to ponder the question Shantell posed to her. She soon realized that it wasn't fair for her to jeopardize the lives of two innocent people,. Not because she had made such a poor choice in men. No matter how she looked at it, Dee-Dee saw no right in it.

"Alright, I'm going to get dressed and head down to the police station. I'm going to take out an order of protection against that motherfucker."

Quietly, Shantell was relieved that Dee-Dee had finally taken a stance against Mario. She felt nothing short of the police would stop this guy. To her, Mario was a ticking time bomb, just waiting to explode.

Dee-Dee got dressed and headed out the door. Her destination was the nearest police station. As soon as she got close to her car, she noticed another note had been placed on it. To her that could only mean one thing: Mario now knew where she lived. She perished the thought.

After removing the note, Dee-Dee quickly read it. She slowly mouthed the words.

"Love is patient, love is kind. It doesn't envy, it doesn't boast, it is not proud. It is not rude, it is not self-seeking, it is not easily angered, it keeps no records of wrongs. Love does not delight in evil but rejoices with the truth. I thought you loved me? At least that's what you said."

When she was done, Dee-Dee began to take a quick inventory of her surroundings. She became paranoid, as if Mario was lurking nearby in the bushes or behind a car.

She couldn't decipher what the poem really meant. All she knew was that Mario was really giving her a bad vibe. Dee-Dee shoved the note into her pocket and hopped into her car and drove off. She planned on showing the note to the police. This was the proof she needed.

Had Dee-Dee bothered to look behind her, she might have seen Mario following closely behind her. The dark shades and baseball cap he wore would have fooled no one, least of all Dee-Dee.

❧

A few weeks later, the restraining order had done little or nothing to curtail Mario's stalking. He still spied on Dee-Dee whenever he felt like it. In fact, his stalking had increased since he was forbidden to make contact with her by phone or come within five hundred feet of her. It was safe to say that all the restraining order did was piss him off.

From his car, Mario watched the apartment with earnest. He took note of all the movement inside. He watched the silhouettes as they passed by the windows and the switching off and on of the lights whenever someone entered or left a room. Mario paid attention to all that and then some. He sat in his car watching and waiting for his turn to strike.

The hot water from the shower was almost scalding hot. When Shantell opened the door she was greeted by a thick cloud of steam. She knew Dee-Dee liked hot showers, but this was ridiculous. She could barely see the shower curtain in front of her.

"Dee-Dee! Dee-Dee!" She called out. "Let me hold the keys to your car so I can drop Jordan off at the baby sitter. You hear me?"

Shantell stood there for a few seconds, waiting for a reply, but none came. Finally, she pulled the shower curtain back and violated Dee-Dee's privacy.

Dee-Dee jumped at the sudden sight of Shantell. Quickly she got into a fighting stance. Her nerves had been shot for the past few weeks, ever since Mario got served with his restraining order. Lord only knew where he was going to pop up next.

"Oh shit!" Dee-Dee exclaimed. "You scared the shit outta me."

"You didn't hear me calling out yo' name?" Shantell explained. "I need yo' keys real quick. I gotta go drop the baby off."

"My keys are on the dresser in my room. They right beside my purse."

"Alright, I'll be right back," Shantell shouted.

When the shower curtain closed, Dee-Dee went right back to meditating. The hot water soothed her, causing Dee-Dee to fall back into a deep state of relaxation. She was zoned out. For the moment, Mario didn't exist.

With all the noise that the shower made, Dee-Dee never heard the apartment door open. She was lost in her thoughts.

Mario must've gone over his plan in his head a thousand times. He had it all figured out. He would break in the apartment and talk to Dee-Dee while her friend wasn't around. He didn't need any outside interference; this was between her and him. If only he could just talk to her, face to face, surely she would drop the restraining order and take him back.

Undetected Mario silently crept through the house. He already watched Shantell and the baby leave the house so he knew that the apartment was empty, with the exception of Dee-Dee.

The loud sounds of running water alerted Mario to Dee-Dee's whereabouts. Slowly he inched his way towards the bathroom door. He was extra careful not to make any unnecessary noise. Mario took small, calculated steps until he reached his destination. As he placed his ear to the door, suddenly the shower water stopped running. Mario backed away from the door and pressed his body flat up against the wall.

Inside the bathroom, Dee-Dee was oblivious to Mario's presence. She continued to tend to her personal hygiene. She applied lotions and deodorant to her body. Dee-Dee even hummed a few songs. For the moment, she was carefree. Soon all that would change.

Dee-Dee wrapped her body in a big fluffy white towel, covering her private parts, then she exited the bathroom. Mario remained motionless as she stepped into the hallway. Then, without warning, Mario sprung out of the shadows.

As soon as he grabbed her arm, Dee-Dee literally jumped. She placed one hand on her heart and paused. Slowly she turned around. Dee-Dee prayed this was Shantell playing around with her. The firmness of the mysterious person's grip told her otherwise.

"Mario?" she spat. "How you get in here?"   Dee-Dee was so frightened that was all she could manage to say at the moment. She was paralyzed by fear.

Mario grabbed Dee-Dee by her arms and slammed her hard up against the wall. He put his face within a fraction of an inch from her face. He spoke through clenched teeth, further emphasizing his anger.

"Don't worry about how I got in here. I got my ways," he warned. "You think some fucking piece of paper is going to stop me? Why you do me like that? Huh? You didn't have to involve the police in our business."

Dee-Dee was in no position to debate with Mario; that might only infuriate him. Wisely she closed her mouth and listened to him rant and rave.

He continued, "That's that bullshit, bitch! You acting real funny lately. You not answering yo' phone. You put The Man on me. What I do to deserve that? Huh? All I did was loved you, with your ungrateful ass."

Suddenly Mario removed a black semi-automatic pistol from his waistband. He pressed the barrel of the gun to Dee-Dee's temple. As he spoke, he jabbed her harder and harder with the gun, as if to emphasize a point.

By this time Dee-Dee began to fear for her life. She didn't know what was coming next. If Mario followed his recent pattern of violence, then she was a dead woman. Dee-Dee decided she wasn't about to wait around. If she was going to die, then she wasn't going down without a fight.

Without warning, Dee-Dee kneed Mario hard in his nuts. Simultaneously, as pain raced through Mario's body and he began to double over in pain, he accidentally pulled the trigger of his gun. A loud shot rang out, the sound echoed inside Mario's head and Dee-Dee slumped to the floor. She died instantly.

Mario looked down at his bloodied lover. He was horrified at what he had just done. He was overcome by a sickening feeling. Sure Mario threatened to kill Dee-Dee,, but there was no way he would have carried it out. He only wanted to talk to her and maybe scare her with the gun. He never imagined something like this would happen.

Mario's mind began to race with mass confusion. He didn't know what he was going to do now; all he knew was he was in deep trouble. Quickly Mario weighted his options before he suddenly realized that his options weren't options at all. There were only two ways out of the situation. Faced with a stiff prison sentence that Mario knew he couldn't do, Mario put the gun to his temple and blew out his brains. He figured he would be with Dee-Dee in death, just as he had in life.

෴

A dizzying blur of red and blue lights blinded Shantell. The large police squad alerted her that something was very wrong. She wondered what the hell had happened at her apartment building. She was only gone twenty minutes and when she returned, half of the Charlotte-Mecklenburg police department was in her apartment complex.

As Shantell moved closer to her building, her progress was halted by the police.

"Ma'am, you can't go any further. This area is a crime scene, subject to a thorough police investigation," the officer informed her.

"Look, I don't care nothing about that. I live here, Officer," Shantell said. "I just wanna get inside my apartment."

"Ma'am, look, I don't think you understand exactly what's going on here. This building has been the scene of what is believed to be a double homicide. No unauthorized personnel will be granted access."

As Shantell and the officer went back and forth, exchanging words, two people from the county coroner's office wheeled a black body bag by on a gurney. Finally, it hit Shantell that somebody had died in her building. She suddenly stopped talking.

"Excuse me, Officer, what apartment did that happen in?"

"Miss, I'm not at liberty to give out that information." The officer told her. "Why? What apartment do you live in?"

"Apartment L."

"Miss, would you please follow me?"

Shantell was taken to a squad car and told of the murder-suicide involving Dee-Dee and Mario. After that, she was questioned extensively about her and the deceased's relationship. As she underwent questioning, her thoughts and prayers were with Dee-Dee, the person who had been snatched out of her life. Shantell was stunned by the news and yet she was relieved at the same time. Shantell was glad that neither she nor her baby was present in that house, or else they might be dead, too.

≈୨୯৯

A light drizzle began to fall on Shantell's windshield as she slowly drove toward the funeral home. Immediately, she turned on the windshield wiper, which made a loud squeaky noise. She ignored it. She wondered if the rain was a sign from God. Her friend's sudden murder had her feeling real spiritual lately. She took the shift in weather as a sign from God. To her, it was as if the heavens were weeping for Dee-Dee.

Dee-Dee was a special friend to Shantell. She was one of those rare people that put the well being of others first. For that, Shantell would always be eternally grateful. Dee-Dee helped out with Jordan as if she were her own. She made life a whole lot easier for Shantell.

As Shantell drove down Beatties Ford road, she began struggling with her emotions. Tears began to flow freely down her cheeks, slightly ruining her makeup. She pulled over to gather her senses; she didn't want the other people at the funeral home to see her like that. Her grieving was private, but none the less painful.

Dressed in all black, Shantell slipped into the funeral home almost unnoticed. The funeral service had just started so all eyes were glued to the casket. Quietly, Shantell took one of the few empty seats in the back. She sat amongst the dozens of mourners who flocked to King's Funeral Home to pay their last respects. Some people were there to honor a person they never knew. News of Dee-Dee's death sent shock waves through the stripping community, but it didn't cause any strippers to quit their jobs. They all knew that dealing with crazy niggers was a hazard of the job. Sex, money and murder sometimes came with the territory. Still, no dancer in their right mind wanted to meet a violent end to their life like Dee-Dee had. They all came to pay their respects.

The street element was in full effect at the funeral home. Though there were people from all walks of life in attendance, the strippers and thugs seemed to stand out the most. Some were inappropriately dressed, which called attention to them. The guys didn't have the proper dress clothes; some were dressed as if the were going to an after party after the funeral service. Many of the strippers had on tight, revealing clothes, totally out of place for this sober event. As Shantell sat in the back, she scanned the crowd and took notes of all this.

"...May this child's death be a reminder to everyone here today, of just how sacred life is. Young people get it together. Y'all out there, in the streets, killing one another for no reason at all. Get right! Get right with God before it's too late," the preacher said.

Shantell listened to the preacher's eulogy and was momentarily moved. She conceded that at the time of her death, Dee-Dee wasn't living right. But surely heaven would look past that and forgive her.

Outside the church, after the funeral service was over, people began to gather in small groups to both mourn and socialize. Shantell would have none of that;, she waved and kept it moving. As she walked to her car, she thought it was a Goddamn shame that more than half the people at the funeral wouldn't even remember Dee-Dee this time next year. Shantell promised herself she would. There was no doubt in her mind.

Shantell was still reeling from Dee-Dee's death, weeks and months after it actually happened. Not only was it hard to believe her friend was gone, but it was hard to accept. Dee-Dee had become such a big part of Shantell and her daughter's life that there was no way to replace her.

If nothing else, Shantell had plenty of experience dealing with tragedy. Just like she had before, she would, in time, get over Dee-Dee's death. Somehow, some way, she had to. Shantell was a survivor; she had no choice.

CHAPTER 6
DIFFERENT STROKES
FOR DIFFERENT FOLKS

"Good morning, babe," Lisa whispered.

"Hey," Shantell replied, as she rolled over in the bed.

Gazing at her new lover, Shantell suddenly became mushy. She was attracted to Lisa in every way possible, but she wasn't alone. Lisa was so fine that she had that effect on men, too.

Before either one of them knew it, their lips locked and their tongues intertwined for a long passionate kiss. The enjoyment Shantell received just from the kiss sent chills up her spine. A man had never made her feel quite this good. Never.

Truth be told, she had never given any man much of a chance to. After the rape she felt totally different about the opposite sex. No male sex partner she had been intimate with, thus far, ever rocked her world. In fact the only time she, had ever felt like this, was when she was with Brandy. And now she had Lisa someone who really loved her.

These two had met at the strip club. Lisa was a stripper from out of town, Columbia, South Carolina. Since she wasn't from Charlotte, it was easier to vibe with her. Their relationship started off quite innocently; Shantell talked and Lisa listened. Shantell had no idea that Lisa was a lesbian.

It was relatively easy for Lisa to win over Shantell. With Dee-Dee dead and gone, she was very vulnerable. The truth of the matter was that if her friend was alive, then there was no way this relationship would have had room to grow. Dee-Dee wouldn't have let Shantell entertain the idea of being with a lesbian, because she was strictly dickly herself. She wouldn't have stood for it at all.

That was then, this was now. For poor Shantell, it was times hard to imagine just how it all happened. Time and time again, she tried to fight the feeling. She tried to wish away the attraction she had for Lisa, but she couldn't. She often wondered how and why did she feel the way she felt.

Her search for answers pointed directly to those reoccurring bouts with loneliness and depression. Her raw, uncontrolled emotions had once again cast questions about Shantell's sexuality and put it to the test.

A long time ago, the disgusted notion that one use to conjure up whenever one thought about lesbians, didn't apply now. Nowadays, that was the in thing. Lesbians had come from behind closed doors to Main Street, USA.

This was especially true in the strip club environment, where women were basically demeaned by men for their own twisted sexual pleasure,   there; lesbianism is rampant and widely accepted, and sometimes even expected. It was no longer nasty or a curse from God to be gay or bisexual. Suddenly, it was cool. Shantell could attest to that. No one shunned or avoided her when they found out she was involved with Lisa.

Now more than ever, Club Champagne was a refuge for her. For Shantell it became more than her workplace, more than a spot where she made her money. It was an escape. She used the club to run away from all the harsh realities of life, like death and poverty. Initially money was the lure. Now she was so emotionally bankrupt, it would take more than currency to get her out of this debt.

Lisa was an exotic-looking African American female. She had soft womanly features, smooth dark skin, long sexy legs and ample amounts of ass and tits. But it was those alluring, slanted oriental eyes that drew Shantell in. What started out as a platonic friendship slowly blossomed into a monogamous relationship.

Within a week's time, Lisa had moved into Shantell's place. Their relationship went deeper than sex. They were bound together by something else, a strong dislike for men. Men had done them both wrong at one point or another. This became common ground for an uncommon bond. Although Shantell was still confused about men, Lisa had totally sworn off them completely. She promised herself from here on out she would only have relationships exclusively with women.

Lisa represented more than just good sex to Shantell. She became someone who got the punch line in all her jokes. She was someone who liked Shantell's style. She was someone who understood Shantell's struggle. She was someone who accepted her faults, listened to her fears and forgave her mistakes. She was someone who accepted Shantell unconditionally.

Unlike her previous sexual experiences with males, Shantell found pleasure in her sexual encounters with Lisa. Not sometimes but all the time, she was sexually gratified. In the past, she had had sex with men for one of two reasons: for money or just because she thought she had to. Those beliefs stemmed from her current occupation as a stripper and the scarring events that happened earlier in her childhood.

Being with Lisa was a relief as much as it was therapeutic. Shantell instantly connected to the closeness, caring and the soothing emotional feeling that the lesbian lifestyle offered. In no time at all, Lisa became the center of Shantell's existence.

"Damn, that was a wet sloppy kiss," Lisa remarked. "I liked that."

Shantell just blushed. She felt a twinge of guilt. It was if she suddenly realized this was wrong. Like the words of a popular love song once said, "If loving you is wrong, I don't wanna be right." At the moment, that's how she felt.

"You's one sexy muthafucka!" Shantell whispered. "And I'd love to stay in bed wit you all day...but I can't. I gotta go get Jordan ready for school. If she misses that bus, I gotta take her there and I don't feel like foolin' with the traffic goin' downtown this morning."

With that said, Shantell quickly got out of bed. She exited the room and headed toward Jordan's room to prepare her for day care.

Intently, Lisa watched Shantell's backside as she left the room. It caused her to get horny all over again. She swore to herself that she was going tear that pussy up as soon as Jordan left for day care.

و&و

"Damn, Shawty, what you doin' later on tonite?" a customer asked.

Shantell ignored him; she was too busy trying to hurry up and finish the lap dance. Not one to turn down a dollar, she had to let this sexual proposition fall on deaf ears. The way this joker was stinking, she knew it couldn't get any better. Shantell couldn't stomach a funky nigger jumping up and down on top of her.

As Shantell was just about to finish up the lap dance, out of nowhere she felt like somebody was staring at her. Her intuition turned out to be correct. A few feet away from her and to the right, Lisa stood by the bar, giving her the evil eye.

Shantell was so pissed off, she immediately left her customer without collecting any of the fallen bills that the man had lavished her with. She went straight to the bathroom. Out of the corner of her eye she could see Lisa following her. That was good, because Shantell wanted to give her a piece of her mind.

"Why the fuck do you keep doin' that? Huh?" Shantell yelled.

"Doin' what?" Lisa replied.

"Now you wanna play stupid, huh?" Bitch, why you keep starin' at me?"

Seeing how mad Shantell was, Lisa decided to downplay the situation. She didn't want to argue with her. She didn't want to run the risk of falling out with Shantell= and possible losing her. Honestly, she couldn't help but stare. Lisa was extremely jealous and overprotective. Shantell was her woman. To her, she was just protecting her interests.

Lisa figured she could smooth all this out with some hot passionate sex later. In the past, that usually did the trick. It usually made her forget what they were mad about in the first place. But tonight, Lisa wouldn't get off the hook that easily.

"Girl, wasn't nobody even payin' you no mind. You trippin'!" Lisa explained. "I was lookin' at Neesha let this dude finger pop her on the down low."

If she thought Shantell was buying that lame-ass excuse, Lisa had another thing coming. This wasn't the first time something like this had happened. Lisa was constantly cock-blocking on Shantell. There were plenty of times, when the club was packed, that Lisa told some of Shantell's regular customers that she wasn't working that night. As first it was cute, till it started messing up Shantell's money.

As the days, weeks and months had went by, Shantell began to realize that being with Lisa was a big mistake. Now she saw what people meant when they said, to never fool around with someone at your job. For her, it was too much of seeing each other. Shantell began to feel like she was being smothered and she couldn't live like that anymore.

Besides that, Shantell had another reason for breaking it off. She had her daughter to think about. The longer this relationship went on, the harder it would become for her to end it. The older Jordan got, the more deeper and penetrating questions she would ask.

Jordan was already being to wonder why she couldn't sleep in bed with Mommy any more, and why did Mommy kiss her new friend like that?

Though she was her own woman, nobody controlled her or told her what to do. Shantell couldn't put her daughter through that. She couldn't have another child walk up to her daughter and tell her that her mommy was gay or, God forbid, that the child would tease Jordan about it.

A million scenarios ran through Shantell's mind. Clearly, Lisa could see the frustration building on her face. She reached out and grabbed Shantell and tried to comfort her, but Shantell shoved her away.

"Get off me!" she spat. "It's over. You gotta go. When we get back home, pack yo' shit and roll."

"Oh it's like that? It's over, just like that?"

"Yep, bitch, I ain't gay no more!" Shantell remarked. "I was confused. I used to be gay."

Lisa looked at her, puzzled. It was as if Shantell was talking out the side of her neck. She couldn't comprehend a word Shantell was saying.

"Shantell, it don't work like that," Lisa laughed. "You don't "used to be' gay. You used to be Christian, you used to smoke cigarettes or maybe you used to wear weaves. But you don't used to be gay. You stuck wit 'that shit fo' life."

Shantell countered, "Yeah, right! Whatever! Say what you want, but I ain't fuckin' wit you no more."

Lisa was deeply hurt by her last statement. In a short time, she had fallen in love with Shantell. She had a problem accepting the fact that Shantell had cut her off so easily.

"Then just say that," Lisa cried. "Then just say that."

Shantell sat on the sink with mixed emotions. She felt guilty for hurting her lover's feelings, but at the same time she felt liberated. She couldn't tolerate her bullshit another minute. This move was the best, for all parties involved.

Chapter 7
The Come up

Mike Boogie strolled into Peaches and Cream strip club like he owned the joint. His New York swagger was alive and well. It showed up in his everyday mannerisms. Mike was pro New York to a fault. He represented it all day, everyday.

Even in the dimly lit club, Mike was on point. Quickly, he scanned the club for any signs of trouble. Seeing none, he couldn't prevent his eyes from roving around the room. There were a couple of pieces of eye candy that caught his attention. Fine young,, partially clothed black women of all shades, shapes and sizes were on display; a few seductively pranced by. Stopping in his tracks, Mike reached out and playfully slapped an unsuspecting stripper, whom he knew, on her ass cheek.

"Stop," she exclaimed. "Nigga don't put your hands on me."

"Stop playin' Ma!" Mike joked. "When you gonna let me hit dat again, Cinnamon, huh?"

At first Cinnamon was upset; she didn't like anyone touching on her for free. But once she saw who he was, her foul attitude suddenly changed. Immediately she turned around and walked over to Mike Boogie and embraced him.

"Mike! Where you been?" Long time, no see? You went back home or somethin'?"

Returning the love, Mike hugged Cinnamon's back and let his hands fall to her waist, then he slowly caressed her ass.

His action caught the eye of one of the many stocky bouncers that patrolled inside and outside the club. The security guard walked over and issued him a stern warning.

"Ay, my man, there's no touchin' the girls!" he firmly stated.

Mike shot the man a perplexed expression, which said, *Nigger you can't be serious. You know who I am?*

Mike was very popular after being in Charlotte for so long. He knew all of the locals and out of towners. He was so popular, he probably could have run for mayor and won. He knew all the movers and shakers in the criminal realm, and even a few important legit people. Mike was so well connected that he was virtually untouchable.

In his younger days, the bouncer would have had a problem on his hands. Mike might have taken his request the wrong way, which would have probably led to a heated verbal exchange and physical altercation. Mike wasn't a big guy, but he carried a big gun and he loved to pop his pistol. He had a little man's complex; he thought the whole world was trying him.

"Aiight, fam. It's all good," Mike said. "You got dat. Anyway…"

Mike was a stone cold hustler who moved drugs throughout almost every hood in the Queen City. He had discovered this gold mine in the late to mid '90's. It was a distant cousin who put him on to the money-making opportunities in Charlotte. Mike came down for a visit and never left.

At that time, New York City was hot. The governor, mayor and police commissioner were making it hard for a drug dealer to eat. All kinds of tough new drug laws, with stiff penalties, had been enacted in an effort to crack down on drug dealers. It was the perfect time for Mike to leave New York. Mike was on the first thing smoking.

Upon arriving in Charlotte, the first thing he noticed about the Queen city was that it was heavily populated with females. Next to making money, having sex ranked a close second for him. Growing up, most kids played football, basketball or some kind of sport. Not Mike; his hobby was fucking. Getting pussy was his favorite pastime. As a teenager he dealt with women, who were much older than himself. As a result he was well versed in the art of fucking. He had the magic stick and he knew it.

Mike stood at 5'8". His dark brown skin made him appear Indian. His hair was jet black and curly. He was well built. He had a charming personality that came across well with women; there was no doubt he was a ladies man. He also was a party animal.

In the strip club and the streets, Mike's sexual reputation preceded him. Tons of chicks knew his name and his game. Funny thing was, after years of running through countless females, having haters throw dirt on his name and salt in his game, he still was able do his thing.

"Lemmie get some money, Mike. I'm fucked up," Cinnamon complained. "These broke-ass nigger's ain't showin' no love tonight."

Mike wisecracked, "Girl, as fat as that ass is, you should keep some money."

One thing about Mike that everyone who was cool with him knew: if he had it, then you could get it. He was a money-making nigger that spread the love. It was because of this fact that he was so beloved in Charlotte.

He didn't move like the average New Yorker. Mike knew the worst thing in the world to do was to come down south, trying to get all the money and fuck all the women. A country boy would kill you, quick. That statement went for any man, regardless of where he was from. To Mike, passing up some new pussy was harder than passing out money.

"Yo, you got some shit wit' you. Every time I see you, you gotta sob story. I always ended up blessin' you wit' some paper. When you gonna bless me?"

Cinnamon sucked her teeth and pretended to be offended.

Mike smirked, thinking to himself, *"you take yo' clothes off in front of strangers every muthafuckin' day. How can anything I say to you, offend you?"*

"Yo, here." He pressed a Fifty-dollar bill into her hand. "Like I said, can I live? Can I smash dat?"

"Nigger, you remember what happened the last time we fucked,." Cinnamon remarked. "Remember?"

Mike froze and thought hard, but his mind drew a blank. Sometimes he got so drunk, he couldn't remember a thing the morning after; this was one of those times. For the life of him, Mike couldn't recall exactly what happened the last time they were together. One thing he knew for sure was, Cinnamon got hers. That was something one could bet on. He would put his life on it. There was no way in hell he could ever be classified by the ladies' as a minute man.

"Oh, you really don't remember huh?" Cinnamon asked. "Well, let me refresh yo' memory. We were in the Microtel up on Sugar Creek. You got me mine and you got yours. Then you went to the bathroom and all hell broke loose. You started cursing up a storm. Callin' me all kinds of bitches and hoes. You said I was a nasty slut for givin' you some pussy while I was on the rag. I knew I wasn't on my period, so I went in the bathroom to look at the condom, picked it up and held it to the light. Dat's when yo' drunk ass realized that the condom was red. And that wasn't blood. Remember?"

Mike grinned, "Oh yeah. My bad!"

"Yeah, that's what you said that night, too."

"Aiight, so now we even." Mike laughed.

"Mike, we'll get up another time," Cinnamon promised. "I got some business to handle tonight."

"I'm holding you to that," he warned. "The next time I see you, it's on. I ain't tryin' to hear none of that other shit, either."

For the most part, Mike was cool with Cinnamon's decision. He was just trying his hand, seeing what he could get into. He was the type of guy who believed in getting in where you fit in. Being turned down was a small thing to him. Anyway, he already had her. Mike was out there slumming, tonight look for some new pussy.

Taking in his surroundings in the club, Mike knew something was going to pop for him tonight. One thing he knew about women: when one won't, one will. He just had to find that one. One thing Mike was sure of, there was no way in hell he was leaving the club empty handed. No way.

In the VIP area, Shantell was one of many strippers giving lap dances. Most dancers would agree that this was a bad working environment. They only felt that way because, it was too wide open, too many prying eyes were cast upon them. The place was small and crowded, but Shantell had to deal with it. Unlike a lot of strip clubs in Charlotte, Peaches and Cream's VIP section wasn't secluded at all. This made it hard on a scandalous stripper to earn an extra couple dollars by committing some lewd sex act.

This is what Shantell had to deal with ever since she left Lisa. She felt in order to break totally free from Lisa, she had to avoid her. Avoiding Lisa meant working elsewhere, which resulted in her having to grind harder. Suddenly, money was tight.

"Damn, girl, you healthier than all outdoors, I swear!" The fat man admitted. "You dating?"

Seductively Shantell smiled at the stranger she was grinding on. She had no interest in the man whatsoever, only his money; but her smile suggested otherwise. Shantell was the great pretender. She was always able to summon a convincing seductive look whenever she needed to. Shantell understood the name of the game was to put the customer at ease and make him feel attractive, even if they weren't.

"Holla, at me later, Big Daddy," she said. "We'll talk."

Shantell collected her money and fled to the locker
room. She felt something wet on her thigh. If she had to guess,
it was semen. The thought alone repulsed her, so inside the
locker room she wiped herself off with baby wipes and rubbing
alcohol. After changing her outfits she hit the floor again, in an
never-ending search for more money.

Meanwhile, Mike stood in front of the bar, tossing back
drink after drink. He liked the vantage point that the bar offered.
He could view the entire club from there; Mike had a light buzz
going on, though he held his liquor well. Feeling good, Mike
was spitting game at every stripper that passed. He said anything
and everything that came to mind.

"Excuse, me I ain't tryin' to be funny or nuttin', but you
got the perfect dick-suckin' lips. I'm sayin'…"

"Fuck you, nigga!" the stripper spat.

Mike laughed as he watched the stripper stomp off. Dis-
respecting them was recreation to him. He got away with things
in the strip club that he would never dare attempt in the nightclub. Usually, strippers were thick skinned, but they were
strange creatures.

Mike tossed insult after insult, direct and subliminal.
Suddenly, everything changed when he spotted Shantell. He
wasn't about to let her pass or run her away, by saying something stupid. Shantell was his type: young, fine and healthy. To
him, she was new meat. Mike hadn't ever seen her. To make it
plain, he was captivated by her. It was just something about
Shantell that made him want her, at least for the night.

Immediately, he went into stunt mode. Reaching into
his pocket, he grabbed a wad of cash. By the time Shantell
reached him, Mike had a handful of large denomination bills,
spread out like a fan, fanning himself with them.

The sight of the cold, hard cash easily caught Shantell's
attention. She stopped in her tracks.

"It's crazy hot in here, right?" Mike cracked. "Want me
to fan you?"

"Is that for me?" Shantell asked.

"Could be," If you play you cards right."

"I ain't know we were playin' cards," she fired back. "I don't like cards. You never know what card you gettin' till you turn it over."

"That's why it's so fun 'Cause you never know?" Mike replied

"Well if you were in a deck of cards, which one would you be?" Shantell asked.

"The Ace of Spades, 'cause I always come in handy," he suggested. "I'ma good dude. It is whut it is wit me. All night I been tryin' to figure out just whut I gotta say to these broads to make 'em understand I'm real. They been dealin' wit' these lame-ass trick niggers for so long, they don't recognize a real nigger."

Two seconds into the conversation Shantell already knew where this stranger was from:, New York. She had never dealt with a real New Yorker. A lot of dudes in Charlotte claimed that they were from New York, but really weren't. From what Shantell had heard from other strippers, 'New York niggers tricked hard and heavy.

Shantell was from the hood; if one asked her, she would say, she had heard it all. She had seen game in many different forms, many times in the strip club; it was a matter of who had the better game: the stripper or the customer. Shantell knew the truth was sprinkled atop of a lot of game. It was up to her to decipher it, to separate the bullshit from the real shit. She liked what she saw, Mike was different and he had an unusual approach.

"Is some of dat for me?" she repeated.

Shantell decided to call his bluff early, just to see if he would part with some cash. After all, she was at work and she was looking to make some money. She decided that if Mike didn't give her any money, then she had to move on. To her, time was money and she didn't have no time to waste just talking.

"Hun, here you go, Ma," Mike responded. He handed her a one hundred-dollar bill.

Quietly, Shantell was taken back by Mike's simple act of generosity. This was the first time in her life that a male had ever given her money without her performing some sexual act. Though this may have been a small thing to Mike, it was big to her. He scored a lot of points with Shantell for this.

"Damn, you for real?" This is mine?"

Mike proudly announced, "Yeah, you can have it. That's you."

Shantell's overexcitement gave her away. Mike knew he had her now. There was no doubt she was hooked, now he just had to reel her in slowly.

"That's some real shit right there," Shantell gushed. "Nigger's ain't doin' it like that 'round here."

"You ain't never met nobody like me. I'ma real nigger! Yo, you want sumthin' to drink? Anything you want, on me."

"I can't drink." Shantell replied. "They don't allow dancers to drink while they workin'.'"

Suddenly, the bar area started to get crowded. Mike started to feel a little claustrophobic so he grabbed her hand and led Shantell to a nearby table. It was there that they began to really get to know each other on a more personal level.

Their conversation seemed to flow effortlessly. For hours, Mike and Shantell kept each other company. She could see that he had deep pockets, but money wasn't the only thing that kept Shantell there. One thing she loved about him was that Mike was very humorous. He kept her laughing all night long. Mike was a sarcastic bastard with a good sense of humor. With all the tragedy that had surrounded her life, Shantell needed a reason to smile; and Mike was it.

"Nigger, you too good to be true. We been sittin', rappin' and you been givin' me money, but you ain't cracked for no sex. What's up wit' that?" Shantell questioned.

"Yo, you get niggers comin' at you like dat all day, everyday," Mike stated. "Why can't I be different?"

After Mike's statement, they both went silent as his words sunk in. Shantell felt there was some truth in that. Mike was right;, she was getting tired of sex-starved guys trying to get with her every time she walked into the club. That was getting old.

Unfortunately it was all game. Mike was just coming from a different angle. His thing was that everybody had a dream that they were trying to fulfill. Mike just had to find out just what Shantell's aspirations in life were and if she didn't have a dream, he sure would sell her one.

"Yo, whut you doin' right now?" Mike suddenly asked. "Why don't we get up outta here?"

His statement took Shantell by surprise. She usually didn't leave the club with guys. Most of the time, she handled her business in or around the club. She was tempted to take the money and run. Since Mike was so nice and different, plus he still had a knot of money, she decided to take a chance.

"Where we goin'?"

"Look, you comin' or what?"

"Alright, gimmie a minute to get dressed."

Inwardly, Mike smiled to himself as Shantell fell right into his trap. He had succeeded in getting her out of her element.

In a flash, Shantell was gone. She went to the locker and put on her clothes. When she reappeared, they exited club. Shantell drew the stares of a few envious strippers. She knew they would be talking about her ass as soon as she left the club. She saw them but chose to ignore them. Shantell was too broke to care what anyone thought.

Outside the club, Mike's beautiful, shiny platinum, four-door Range Rover Sport seemed to stand out amongst the rest of the vehicles. The SUV was his pride and joy. He pushed a button on his key ring and the Range Rover purred to life.

"This ya' car?" Shantell asked.

"Whut you think? I'm drivin' somebody else's shit?"
Mike snapped. "This is me! Damn, you wanna see my paper-
work?"

Together they climbed inside the car and after fastening
their seatbelts, Mike took off. Carefully he drove through the
city streets. By the way he drove, one could tell he really cared
for his car. He drove like he had nowhere to go. Taking his
time, he avoided all the potholes and speed traps.

While Mike drove, Shantell silently sat relaxed in her
seat. From the passenger's seat she silently admired the SUV's
lavish interior. Needless to say, she was impressed. She had
never been in a car this fancy.

Maneuverings through the city streets, Mike made his
way out of the hood and into upper class neighborhoods. From
her seat, Shantell noticed the change in scenery. Though she was
a resident of Charlotte, born and raised, she wasn't familiar with
this part of town.

Despite her best efforts to remain silent, Shantell
couldn't. She had to know their destination.

"So where we goin'?" She inquired.

"Ma, be easy," Mike suggested. "Sometimes it's not
where you going, but who's taken you'."

Mike's reassurance was enough for Shantell. She didn't
say another word. She decided to go with the flow.

Before long Shantell's patience was rewarded. The couple wound up in somewhere in South Charlotte. The whole
vibe over there was different from the rest of Charlotte. Everything was so clean and beautiful and peaceful.

Through the tinted windows, Shantell caught a glimpse
of South Park Mall. As they cruised along Sharon road, suddenly
Mike took a left onto Colony Road. If Shantell knew where
they were going before, she didn't know now.

After taking a quick right, Mike had finally reached his
destination. Shantell was awestruck at what she saw; it was
beautiful.

In the middle of a large fountain, there was a huge, aqua-green-colored statue of two bald eagles with their wings spread wide. The artist captured them beautifully; they appeared to be soaring.

Shantell was mesmerized by the statue and the water which it sat in. After Mike parked, she got out the car to get a closer look. Though she had lived in Charlotte all her life, Shantell didn't know that this spot existed. Mike had scored even more points with her. She hadn't known him three hours and already he had shown her a whole different world.

In almost anyone's opinion, this place was breathtaking. It was well lit and with pockets of darkness surrounding the fountain. The water itself was nicely lit. This was the kind of place one would bring a lover. Mike knew Shantell would enjoy the ambiance of the place.

As Shantell sat on the water's edge, Mike slid up on her and sat close besides her. He was preparing himself to make his sales pitch. He was really going to get up close and personal.

"Shantell whut is it that you want out of life? You know you can't dance forever? You got any plans?"

Though his line of question was small, his words pierced Shantell's soul. He touched her. Nobody had ever bothered to ask her what she wanted to do with herself.

"To tell you the truth, Mike, I don't even know. Right now, I'm just tryin' to feed my daughter. As long as she alright, I'm alright."

"You got any hidden talents? Any hobbies?" Mike inquired. "Somethin' you love ta do, or would do for nuttin'?"

Shantell didn't have to think long; immediately one thing came to mind. Shantell loved to sing. It wasn't something she thought she could do it was something she knew she could do. Throughout her young life Shantell had sung. She sung when she was happy and when she was sad.

"Yeah, I do a little singing."

"Oh, yeah? Well, check this out. I gotta partner of mine named Sowell. Him and his brother O own a club called Studio

74. Every Monday night they have a little amateur night contest for rappers and singers. I'ma give him a call and get you up on that stage."

"For real?" She responded excitingly. "You'd do that for me?"

Shantell didn't doubt that Mike was well connected. After all, he had some of the earmarks of success. He had money and an expensive car.

"Of course I would. I'm here to help you, not hurt you. Who am I to kill your dream?"

Mike looked into Shantell's eyes. "My moms always told me, there are two kinds of people that are gonna enter yo' life, givers and takers. Think about it. When somebody comes into yo' life, they either gonna put food on yo' table or take something off."

Even if Shantell didn't say it verbally, she had to admit that Mike had a point. There was no denying it, either.

"Well, I'm the type of nigger dat's gonna put somethin' on yo' table!"

From that point on, Shantell was putty in Mike's hands. He was inside her head, dominating her every thought. She had visions of being with him. To her, he was the one.

Sitting by the water's edge, Shantell was deep in thought. The only thing breaking the silence was the light splashing of water. Meanwhile, Mike Boogie was growing steadily impatient. Slyly he glanced down at his watch; it would be morning soon. He felt now was the time to make his move.

"Shantell I ain't even going to lie to you." he stated. "I'm crazy attracted to you."

Mike put his arms around her, pulling her close. Then he seductively whispered in her ear.

"You so fuckin' fine, I just want to taste you."

Mike had played his cards right all night. He knew that no woman in her right mind would resist the chance to receive oral sex, and not have to give up anything.

Shantell bit her lip seductively; Mike's offer was definitely inviting. There was no doubt that she was attracted to him. But at this point, Shantell felt like she owed him. She didn't want to turn him down. In her mind, it was only right to let him do it. Besides that this was going to be sexually gratifying to her.

"All you wanna do is eat it, right?"

"Dat's all I wanna do, Ma," Mike replied. "Make you feel good."

Mike wasn't in the habit of giving strippers oral sex, but he wanted Shantell so bad, he'd say anything to get in her pants.

Leading her back to his truck, Mike held Shantell's hand as they stepped on the loose gravel that surrounded the fountain and made their way to the parking lot. As soon as they reached the car, they climbed into the back seat. That's when Mike went to work.

Quickly, he unfastened her skin tight jeans. Shantell lifted herself off the seat so he could pull her pants down to her ankles. Once that was done he dived right in.

Once on his knees, Mike buried his head between her legs. There, he was greeted by the fresh scent of a clean vagina. With two fingers, on each hand, he opened her vagina and began to hungrily bite, lick, and suck on her clitoris.

Cries of passion escaped from Shantell's lips as she came closer and closer to a climax. The windows began to fog up from all the heat these two generated. During the heat of the moment, Mike stopped giving her oral sex. Smoothly he unzipped his pants and inserted in penis inside Shantell. Despite the fact that they were having unprotected sex, Shantell went with the program. It was just as good for her as it was for him.

The young vagina seemed to grab at Mike's penis with each thrust from his hips. Mike was getting more than he bargained for. It was hard for him to keep from climaxing. He had to block the actual act of sex from his mind. He replaced it with thoughts of the police, of all things. He began to look around for them because if he got caught having sex in his car in these white people's neighborhood, then they were going to jail, for sure.

Mike had a hell of a time focusing on sex and keeping an eye open for the police. In his mind, he was putting it on Shantell but she was giving him the business, too. Unable to take it anymore, Shantell violently climaxed. Just before Mike came he pulled out, ejaculating somewhere on the floor.

It was then that Mike came to his senses. He began to worry about all the damage they had done to the interior of his new car. He promised himself to get it thoroughly detailed tomorrow.

This was their very first sexual encounter, but one wouldn't know it by the way they just went at it. It left them both fulfilled yet yearning for more. Their sexual response and performance assured that Mike and Shantell would see each other again.

"Yo, hurry up and get yourself together," Mike insisted. "Let's get the fuck up outta here 'fore the police come."

"You droppin' me off, right?" Shantell asked.

"Yeah. What am I'm supposed to do, leave you here?" Mike shook his head. "Yo, I don't know what type of niggers you been dealin' with, but I ain't foul like that."

The minute she uttered the words, Shantell regretted it. To her, getting dropped off wasn't a given. She had sex with plenty of guys who, when they were done, went about their business. Getting treated well by a man was something Shantell wasn't used to. Soon, all of that would change.

"Yo, what you doin' tomorrow?" Mike asked.

"Probably, sleep till the afternoon. Then I'm going and picking up my daughter from the babysitter."

"Aiight, look. After you get up, call me. I'll take you to go get your daughter, then we'll go shoppin' at Concord Mills Mall."

That sounded like a plan to Shantell. She was going to definitely do that. If Mike wanted to look out for her, then she was going to let him. Financially, she was in no position to turn anything down.

CHAPTER 8
MUST BE NICE

"With the fifth pick in the draft, the Charlotte Bobcats select Ronald Wright from Duke University." the NBA commissioner announced.

The cameras quickly panned to the draftee's table. There a tall, clean-cut, African American male in an expensive Italian suit, stood up. He hugged and kissed his mom and dad before he elegantly walked up on the stage. He donned his team's cap, shook Commissioner Stern's hand, and poised for pictures. On the big screen, his collegiate highlights played for a group of basketball fans.

Veteran NBA announcers sung the young's man's praise. "Good, solid pick, one said. "Here's a young man who doesn't have any questionable character issues surrounding him. It's highly unlikely that he'll do anything to embarrass himself, his family or his organization."

"I agree with you on that, Charles," another announcer spoke. "But besides all that, the kid is a beast. He can score at will. To me, he's in the same class as the Carmelo Anthony's, the Kobe Bryant's, The Dwayne Wades and the Lebron James's of the league. Meaning, this kid is an impact player."

At 6'6", 230 lbs., Ronald Wright was labeled a "can't miss" prospect. His sophomore season in the Atlantic Coast Conference, he averaged 24.5 points per game and 4.7 assists per game while grabbing 6.3 rebounds per game. On his way to winning Atlantic Coast Conference Player of the Year honors as

well as National Player of the Year honors, he led the Blue
Devils to another national championship.

This was a player who could play three positions: point
guard, shooting guard and small forward. Ronald was a multi-
talented kid who could take over all facets of the game. Coming
out of a winning program like Duke only made him that much
more attractive to NBA franchises. Some felt he was the best
player and purest athlete in the draft.

At the pre-draft camp in Portsmouth, Virginia and in
personal workouts, Ronald Wright had left a strong impression
on the NBA scouts and general mangers. They raved over his
court awareness and the poise he possessed for such a young
player.

The only reason he didn't go higher in the draft was because it was loaded with foreign players and big men. These
were the two hottest commodities. Unfortunately for Ronald
Wright, he was neither. To NBA scouts, foreign-born NBA
players came into the league more polished than their American
counterparts. True centers and power forwards were thought to
be rare. In the NBA, some ideologies die hard. It was said," You
can't teach height."

Ronald Wright was a rare player: he was a suburb kid
with an inner-city street game. He would make the five other
NBA teams that passed on his services, one day regret it. This
young man had the hopes of the entire city of Charlotte on his
young shoulders. From day one, he was hailed as a savior.

The Bobcat Arena is beautiful, nineteen thousand-seat,
state-of-the-art arena, owned by African American billionaire
Bob Johnson and part owner Michael Jordan. The team is in its
third year of existence. For the city of Charlotte, this is its
second NBA team. Their first team, the Charlotte Hornets,
moved from the city and had been led by an unscrupulous
owner, George Shinn. Embarrassed by one of its own, the NBA
rectified the situation by awarding the people of Charlotte an
expansion team a few years later.

There were high expectations for the Bobcats in year three. They had drafted well in the recent years, acquiring good young talent like point guard Raymond Felton, power forwards Emeka Okafor and Sean May. Now, with the addition of Ronald Wright, on paper, the future looked bright.

Success on the collegiate level didn't go to Ronald Wright's head. Immediately after the draft he hired a personal trainer, a chef, and embarked on a serious workout program. He wanted to gain the edge on the competition. Ronald knew that his God-given talents were nothing without the gift, but his gift was nothing without hard work.

Going from college to the pros was huge adjustment for any athlete. There were things happening around the league that college just didn't prepare one for, like dealing with large sums of money and gold-digging women. Dorothy Wright was familiar with the horror stories. To keep the wolves at bay, she decided to move with her son to Charlotte, to watch over him like she always had. She was an overbearing mom who had never severed the umbilical cord. No matter how old Ronald got or how many millions he made, he would always be her baby.

Dorothy Wright was a college-educated professional who worked as a principal in a small town in Connecticut. She knew the value of a good education and money. That's why she pressured her son into accepting an athletic scholarship to Duke University. Though she was dead set against her son leaving school after his sophomore year, she looked at his entrance into the draft as a career move. She made Ronald sign a contract promising to return to school and get his degree, sometime in the near future.

Absent from Ronald Wright's circle were the large entourages that usually accompanied NBA players. Another thing one wouldn't associate with Ronald Wright was bling bling, especially large platinum chains with diamond-encrusted pendants. His mother kept him free from all of that non-sense. As far as Dorothy was concerned, her son was a commodity. It was her job to capitalize off his clean, wholesome image. She had an image to sell to corporate America. This was a business, and she was going to treat it as such.

☙❧

"Yeah, I knew it. I knew the Bobcats were gonna pick this nigger," Mike happily said. "Money got a serious game."

From the comforts of Shantell's living room, Mike intently watched the draft. Though Mike was a die-hard New York Knicks fan, secretly he had adopted the Charlotte Bobcats as his new favorite team, what with the Knicks organization in turmoil.

It was then that Shantell's eyes were drawn to the television. She looked up at the tall young man on the television with the pearly white, mega watt smile, and had to admit he was strikingly handsome.

"So this is the next Michael Jordan, huh?"

Shantell wasn't a big sports fan, but she knew a little something about basketball, from her brother. Quietly she would be glad when the NBA a draft was over. It was cutting into her television time. In a few minutes, reruns of her favorite program, *Flavor of Love*, would be on. Ever though she saw it Sunday, she wanted to see it again.

But as long as the NBA draft was on, it wasn't in her immediate future. Mike was glued to the television, like every real basketball fan. To them, the draft was special, no matter how bad your team was doing; after the draft, one believed that they would do better. No matter that these kids were drafted on potential and they hadn't done a thing in the league yet; that didn't mean a thing.

All this meant to Shantell was that her best television, the high-definition big screen TV was temporarily on lock down. Her daughter was watching cartoons on the other TV in her room. Shantell could live with that, since it was Mike who bought the television in the first place.

Since meeting Mike, Shantell's fortunes had changed. Things just kept getting better and better for her. She had gone from virtually struggling to doing good, all thanks to Mike's presence. Once he really got to know Shantell, he made his intentions clear. He explained to her his situation, meaning he had a girlfriend and he wasn't leaving her. He told Shantell, 'You know about her, but she doesn't know about you.' Shantell knew she couldn't really be seen in public with Mike, but in exchange for her accepting his situation, he would take care of her financially. Of course, all this was provided that she kept him satisfied sexually.

The fact that she had a mouth to feed weighed heavily on Shantell's decision to accept his indecent proposal. Quickly she learned that she would have to do more than bed Mike to earn her keep. And she learned exactly how Mike made a living.

Mike was the leader of a large-scale drug operation. He used Shantell's home as a stash house. Mike had moved her out of her old neighborhood and tucked her in a nice, gated apartment complex in the university area of Charlotte. In exchange for her turning a blind eye to his drug activities, Mike took care of her and the baby.

Their relationship was far from perfect. Mike was promiscuous and Shantell was needy. She not only needed money, but more importantly, she needed time and Mike's undivided attention, something she would never get. Shantell came into the situation understanding her position, but as the relationship progressed, she wanted to change the game.

CHAPTER 9
GETTING IT TOGETHER

God grant me the strength to accept the things I cannot change, and the courage to change the things I can, and the wisdom to know the difference, Brenda mentally recited the Serenity Prayer.

For the first time in a long time, Brenda Bryant was at peace. She had broken the heavy shackles of dependency that cocaine had placed upon her. After being sentenced to six months in the county jail, of which she served about ninety days, Brenda was court ordered to a drug rehab facility somewhere in the mountains of North Carolina. This distraction-free environment was the perfect place for her to detox.

Unlike a lot of other users, Brenda didn't enter the drug program in an attempt to beat the system. This wasn't an get-out-of–jail-free pass to her. She needed help and more importantly, she wanted it. For her, this was the first step in her long road to recovery. This was a step in the right direction for Brenda.

At this inpatient program, Brenda endured a rigorous daily schedule of one-on-one drug counseling, group meetings, and psychological evaluations. Every day she received large doses of in-depth drug and alcohol education. Brenda came into contact with addicts, fiends and junkies from all walks of life and from every racial denomination. It was here she realized just how widespread drug usage was. She also realized that using drugs wasn't an addiction, but a disease.

Brenda realized that breaking her drug addiction would be difficult, but not impossible. She had to slow down and take life one day at a time. The answers to life's mysteries were not inside a crack cocaine rock.

These were the twelve longest weeks of her life. Brenda was forced to take a long, hard look at herself. She was forced to confront the consequences of her drug use, her life and what she had become. She had denied her drug use to a lot of people in the past, but now she couldn't lie to herself.

By confronting one of the toughest challenges of her life, Brenda found out a lot about herself. She learned just how strong and resilient she was. As a direct result she began to feel terrible about the way she had neglected her kids. She blamed herself for her kid's bad choices in life. Brenda felt that she was at fault for her son's lengthy incarceration and Shantell's new occupation as stripper. Though she never mentioned it to her daughter, Brenda knew. She had heard about Shantell on the street. The streets were always watching and people were always running their mouths.

Brenda went on a guilt trip until counselors and members of her group pulled her out of it. They reassured her that many people had done far worse things than neglect while in their state of addiction. This allowed Brenda to put things in perspective.

To Brenda, being arrested was god-sent. Jail had succeeded in nursing her body back to health. She quickly regained her weight and started looking like the Brenda of old. Now it was up to the drug facility to mend her mind, to make her whole again.

As she embarked on her soul-searching mission, Brenda realized that she had the power to change her life. The drug rehab helped her see things more clearly and it helped her get her priorities in order. She only hoped it wasn't too late to reconcile with her children.

Brenda had already lost one child to the streets; she would be damned if she would lose another. From rehab she began to write her daughter many apology letters, in hopes of some sort of closure to the matter. She hoped that Shantell would forgive her and most of all, that her invitation was still open. Because quite frankly, whenever this program was finished, she had nowhere to go. Her best bet was a city shelter. Brenda knew if she went back to the hood, then surely she would relapse. With the drug problem the way it was in the Black community, drugs were everywhere; the temptation would just be too great to overcome.

❧

In the wee hours of the morning, the Greyhound exited the highway ramp and rambled through uptown Charlotte towards it destination, the bus station. Most of the passengers were fast asleep, but not Brenda. She was wide-eyed, taking in the scenery. Though she had only been gone less than a year, it felt like an eon to her. Brenda wasn't a hardened criminal who was used to being locked down. Having her freedom snatched from her was a traumatic experience for Brenda,. One she didn't want to relive anytime soon.

The bus driver flicked on the bus' interior lights; this signaled the end of the ride for her. Brenda was back home. Finally, she was free.

When Brenda stepped off the bus, she took a deep breath and smiled. She never realized how good polluted air was. While she waited for her luggage, she gazed up at the stars in the sky. Brenda shook her head at the wonder of the universe. Never before in her life had the little things meant so much.

"Ma," a voice called out. "Over here."

Recognizing the voice, Brenda spun around and looked for her daughter. There, in the doorway, she saw Shantell and Jordan madly waving. All things considered, this greeting was beautiful, like a ticker tape parade. Suddenly Brenda got emotional and a tear trickled down her cheek.

While the bus was en route to Charlotte, Brenda wondered what a moment like this might do to her. Now she knew. She walked over and embraced her family.

"God is good," she thought.

"Ma, you look real good." Shantell insisted. "I'm so glad you're home! We got a lot of catchin' up to do."

"We sure do," Brenda agreed. "You have to fill me in on everything that's goin' on with you and my grandbaby here."

Brenda reached down and picked up her granddaughter. Words couldn't explain how happy she was when Jordan not only came to her but stayed in her arms. This was a moment Shantell had been waiting for, for years. She hoped it was a sign of things to come.

After gathering Brenda's suitcase, the trio piled inside Shantell's brand new black Honda Accord and headed home.

Shantell and Brenda made small talk as she drove. Meanwhile, in the back seat, Jordan fell fast asleep inside her car seat.

"Where you get this bad car from?" her mother questioned. "Must have cost you a pretty penny, huh?"

Shantell wasn't used to answering to anybody, least of all her mother. Brenda's line of questioning had caught her off guard. She knew her mother wasn't stupid; you couldn't just tell her anything and expect her to believe it. Shantell decided to tell her the truth. She only hoped that her mother would extend her the same courtesy.

"My friend bought it for me. I don't know how much it costs. I'm really not into cars."

"Your friend?" Brenda commented. "What kinda friend buys you expensive things like this? Is he your boyfriend? What does he do for a living?"

Goddamn you nosey! Shantell thought. *Here we go.*

They hadn't been reunited ten minutes, and already Brenda was back to her old self. She was back to being a concerned parent and Shantell didn't like it one bit. She wasn't a little kid any more. She was grown, with a daughter of her own. Who was her mother to be questioning her, anyway?

Instead of verbally communicating her thoughts, Shantell took a more diplomatic approach. She bit her tongue.

"He's just a friend. Nuttin' more and nuttin' less." Brenda could sense that her daughter didn't want to speak about the car anymore, so she dropped the subject. She knew that one day she would eventually meet this mystery man, then she would get a chance to pose all her questions directly to him.

Soon the ride was over. Shantell and her mother exited the car; they gathered up the baby and her things and entered the apartment. After tucking her daughter into bed, Shantell showed her mother the apartment.

The first thing that crossed Brenda's mind was, *God damn! How in the hell can my daughter afford such a nice place?*

Though Brenda was a God-fearing woman, her daughter's apartment was so nicely furnished and decorated that it provoked her to use profanity.

She peeked into the living room and saw the butter-soft, walnut brown leather couch, with matching love seat and recliner, and the big screen television. It seemed like every modern electric appliance was on display at Shantell's home.

Next Brenda saw her massive cherry oak, king-sized bed and her expensive, ultra-soft pillow top mattress. On Shantell's wall was a 42-inch plasma television and numerous hand-painted portraits of the dead rappers Tupac Shakur and Biggie Smalls.

When the two women reached the spare room, there was no let down in luxury. Shantell had basically furnished the room the same way, with one exception: her mother had a 20-inch flat screen on her night table instead of a plasma television hanging on her wall.

"You hungry Ma?" Shantell asked.

"No, I'm alright. I'm too happy to be hungry," Brenda remarked.

"Okay, then. I'm goin' to go lay down. Yo' granddaughter is a handful. I need my rest."

"Don't go yet, Shantell. Sit on the bed and let's talk for awhile," Brenda suggested.

Though Shantell didn't initiate the conversation, she welcomed it wholeheartedly. She was dying to hear just what her mother had to say. She came back and sat on the bed.

Brenda began, "Shantell, I ain't gotta tell you I ain't been the best mother in the world. You already know that. I feel so sorry about how things went between you and me. The drugs got a hold of me and wouldn't let go. I just wanted you to know that that lady wasn't your mother. I don't know who that imposter was, but it wasn't me. I apologize to you. I hope you can accept my apology."

Before the words were completely out of her mouth, Brenda began to cry. This heart-to-heart talk had opened up a floodgate of tears. Brenda's body was racked by loud sobs and sniffling.

It was then that Shantell reached out to her mother and pulled her close to hug her. Silently she reassured Brenda that everything was alright.

"Don't worry about it, Ma. That was then, this is now. We all make mistakes. Nobody walkin' this earth is perfect. I forgive you, Ma,"

By consoling her guilt-ridden mother, Shantell went a long way in reestablishing their bond. Shantell couldn't help but shed a tear or two in the process. Only these tears were different than the ones from years gone by. They were tears of joy, not tears of pain and frustration.

As the days and weeks went by, these two had more and more frequent candid conversations. Brenda learned a lot about her daughter and vice versa. It was during one of these talks that Brenda would learn something she didn't care to ever know.

"Shantell, how about me, you and Jordan take a trip to the jail to go see you brother, Reggie?" Brenda suggested. "I haven't seen my son in years, and I feel real bad about it. I don't know where I went wrong with that boy."

"I don't know why you feel so bad about it," Shantell snapped. "You ain't put him there. He put his own self there. Yo' son was not a very good person."

Brenda was dumbfounded. She couldn't believe her daughter could be so cold-hearted to her own brother. She thought she raised her better than that.

"Shantell, don't talk like that," Brenda warned. "That's your brother, you know. Have a heart."

"Reggie ain't no brother of mine. He ain't nobody to me," Shantell stated flatly. "I ain't got no brother."

Desperately, Brenda looked into Shantell eyes for signs of a prank. She hoped this was some kind of practical joke, but it wasn't. Her daughter's eyes didn't lie; they were alive with hatred.

Shantell wasn't pulling any punches when it came to Reggie. Now it was time to let the world know what happened in that house that day. Why should she keep it to herself? Just for the stake of harmony? Shantell thought an act as dastardly as that deserved to be exposed.

"Shantell, what's wrong with you, huh?" her mother said.

"You wanna know what's wrong with me? Huh? You really wanna know what's wrong with me? Yo' son, Reggie, raped me!"

"What?!" Brenda replied in disbelief.

"You heard me." Shantell barked.

Brenda was devastated by the news. *This couldn't be true*, she thought. All at once, her mind began to overflow with questions of how, why and when? These were questions she had no logical answers to. Only Shantell could provide the specifics, and that she did.

Stone–faced, Shantell bravely recounted the rape, the time and date in which the incident took place. She filled in all the blanks. Her vivid recollection left little to the imagination. While describing what her brother did to her, sometimes she laughed to keep from crying.

Brenda was stunned by the story she just heard. This was a bitter pill for her to swallow. She never knew a child of hers was capable of such savagery. Although Brenda more than sympathized with her daughter she knew that the information Shantell supplied her with was like a death sentence, as far as the family was concerned. Any illusions Brenda had about them being one big happy family, died that day. Things would never be the same.

Now that she had finally told her mother, Shantell felt like a burden was lifted off her shoulders. She closed the book on an ugly chapter in her life. She didn't care how her mother dealt with the situation; that was on her. If she still wanted a relationship with her brother it was up to her. As far as Shantell was concerned, Reggie didn't even exist any more.

It took days for the initial shock to wear off. Brenda was smart enough to realize there was nothing she could ever say in Reggie's defense. As much as she would have loved to defend any one of her children against any allegation, Reggie had done the unthinkable, and it left her speechless. Needless to say, this topic would never be revisited. It was now a private matter, a deep dark family secret.

Bbbbbbllllliiinng! Bbbbbbllllliiinng! Bbbbbbllllliiinng!

The house phone rang, breaking the early morning silence.

Shantell heard it but chose to ignore it. She knew it wasn't anybody but Mike, which meant that he wanted something, sex or drugs. Lately, he had become so predictable. Unfortunately for him, Shantell didn't feel like being bothered right now. When she was sleepy, she had a "fuck the world" attitude. Whoever was on the phone, she would deal with them later.

"Shantell! Shantell! The phone," Her mother hollered. "Somebody named Mike wanna speak to you."

As much as Shantell tried to ignore her mother, she couldn't. Momentarily her mother's voice took her back to her childhood, when Brenda used to wake her up early for school. Now Shantell was officially up.

"Yeah. I got it."

Shantell reached over to the night table and fumbled for the phone.

"Hello?" she groggily spoke into the receiver.

"Aye, yo, you sleep?" Mike inquired.

Shantell fired back, "Yeah, why?"

"Yo, I need you to get up and get me two of those things. "I'll be right there inna minute. I'm comin' up West Harris right now." With that said, Mike hung up.

Shantell got up and did as she was told. She went into her closet and retrieved two ounces of crack cocaine from one of her old winter coats. She was glad Mike hadn't asked her to drop it off for him. Lately, he had not been only using her apartment as a drug stash house, but Mike had turned her into a drug courier. At times she would distribute crack to Mike's long list of customers, whenever he asked her to. She was at his beck and call

Due to her involvement in the drug trade, Shantell stopped stripping. She didn't have to; Mike took care of her every need.

More and more, she was becoming complacent; Shantell was relying heavily on Mike. That's how Mike wanted it,; he was a control freak. He loved to have his ladies be totally dependent on him. Literally, he made it hard for them to live without him.

Mike inserted the keys in lock and opened the door. When he entered the apartment, the sudden sight of Brenda, who was sitting in the living room watching television, startled him. Shantell had told him that her mother would be staying with her for a little while, but seeing Brenda was something totally different. Mike was used to having total privacy and the run of the house. After all, he paid all the bills there.

"Oh, hi. How you doin'?" Mike greeted her.

Brenda looked Mike over suspiciously. She hadn't heard him come in. Then it dawned on her; this must be Shantell's "friend."

"Good morning," Brenda politely replied.

Not that Mike was trying to hide it, but Brenda detected his strong New York accent. That, coupled with the way he was dressed in an expensive Wissam leather jacket and long platinum chain with a diamond entrusted crucifix, and Brenda knew he was a dope boy.

Before Brenda could say another word Mike had blown past the living room and entered Shantell's room. Shantell handed him his drugs, he said a few words to her, then left the apartment as fast as he had come. On the way out, he acted like he didn't even see Brenda.

As soon as Mike left, Brenda marched to her daughter's room. Shantell was just about to get back into bed when her mother knocked on the door.

"Come in," she said.

"Shantell, was that your friend?" Brenda questioned her. "Why you didn't introduce us?"

Here comes twenty-one questions, Shantell thought.

"Look, Ma," she began. "He had somewhere to go. He locked his keys in his car and he came over to pick up da spare."

"Oh?" Brenda commented. "Maybe I'll get a chance to meet him next time."

"Maybe," Shantell repeated.

Brenda began to leave the room. Suddenly she stopped in the doorway.

"I know you grown, and this might not be my place to tell you, but I wouldn't be a parent if I didn't tell you this. Leave that boy alone. He got trouble written all over him. I don't know what it is, but somethin' ain't right about him."

Brenda realized that she had just stuck her neck out there, but she didn't care. When it came to her daughter, her job was to protect her at all costs. Brenda may have been guilty of not doing that in the past but the same couldn't be said now.

She knew Shantell might not like her assessment of her friend, but that was the chance she took.

Totally ignoring her mother, Shantell just threw the covers over her head. She didn't bother to reply. She totally disregarded her mother's opinion. She thought Brenda was just being old fashioned.

After all this was her life, she could see whomever she pleased. She was glad her mother had gotten her life together, but now she felt her mother was going too far. Shantell was starting to feel like she couldn't be a woman in her own house.

CHAPTER 10
SIDE CHICK

The Hyatt Hotel, located in South Charlotte, was jam-packed, due to heavy promotion from Power 98 morning show, No Limit Larry and Tone X. Anybody who was somebody was there, and the women and men were dressed to impress. This was the party of the year, by far. This party was thrown by Adolph Shiver, the number one party promoter. When Adolph threw a party it was more like an event, anticipated by all, for weeks ahead of time.

Even though Shantell wasn't in that party-going crowd, she had heard of Adolph. She was surprised when Mike had come by earlier and given her a VIP pass to the party. Mike had never taken her anywhere but the hotel so when he extended her this invitation, Shantell jumped at the opportunity to go out on a real date with him.

Standing in the full-length mirror, Shantell thoroughly inspected herself. She turned from side to side, then she looked front to back. She was quite satisfied with her appearance. Her black, form-fitting corset dress from BeBe, complimented her hourglass figure. In this dress, she had hips and ass for days. The dress also pushed up her breasts, making them look bigger than they were. The four-and-half-inch studded heels gave Shantell even more sex appeal. She topped the outfit off with a beautiful black mink stole. After donning her Gucci sunglasses, Shantell was just about set.

She walked into the bathroom to apply a little makeup. Shantell wasn't the type who needed to apply tons of makeup. She was naturally beautiful.

"Shantell, you look so nice," Brenda complimented her.

"Thanks," she replied.

Shantell had spent half the day shopping, getting a manicure and pedicure, and getting her hair done. She planned to do more than just turn heads. Tonight, after she was finished, Mike wouldn't ever look at her the same.

"C'mere, Jordan,." Shantell yelled.

Jordan came running out of her room into the bathroom. Shantell was applying eyeliner when she arrived. She finished placing her MAC makeup back in her purse.

"Give Mommy a kiss," she commanded.

Jordan got up on her tiptoes and Shantell leaned over. They met at a halfway point and exchanged kisses, then quickly Shantell hugged her.

"Be good for Grandma, alright? Don't be a bad girl."

"I won't," Jordan promised.

"Okay. I gotta go. I love you."

"I love you," Jordan repeated.

Shantell put her daughter down and headed for the front door. As she passed the living room she saw her mother channel surfing with the remote control. Brenda paused for a moment and looked at Shantell.

"Shantell, what time you think you'll be back in?"

Here we go again, Shantell thought.

"I don't know. "Why?"

"Oh, I was just asking," Brenda said defensively.

Shantell promised herself she was going to have a talk with her mother about getting a job. Her mother had way too much time on her hands and she was using most of it to get in her business. Shantell felt that her mother needed to get a life, maybe find a boyfriend or something. She was really beginning to irk the hell out of her. It was sad to say, but the apartment was becoming too small for the both of them.

"Don't wait up," Shantell suggested.

Brenda brushed aside her daughter's snide remark. She went back to watching television. Unfortunately for her, there wasn't a decent movie on cable, so Brenda got up and began cleaning up the house. This was one of the good habits she picked up while incarcerated.

One thing about Brenda, she didn't mind cleaning up around her daughter's apartment. She had been a domestic most of her life. She figured it was the least she could do to earn her keep.

First she straightened up the living room. She dusted the ceiling fan, then she cleaned off the glass tables, and the big screen television. Finally she worked her way to the kitchen, and then to Shantell's room.

"Jordan go watch TV in the living room, Let Grandma clean up in here."

"Okay," Jordan answered.

Watching her granddaughter bounce out the room, Brenda couldn't help but wonder what the child was doing up this late at night. In her day, children were placed on schedules, even forced to go to sleep. But not now; now, kids had more rights than a little bit. Brenda dared not interfere with her daughter's raising of her child. She knew from experience that people were funny about their kids, even family.

Starting with the bed, Brenda began systematically fixing up the room. She took the clothes that had been thrown on the floor and put them in the hamper. She put fresh sheets on the bed and made it up. Then she hung up all the outfits that Shantell had tried on tonight and discarded around the room.

Before Brenda knew it, her work was complete. She stood at her daughter's closet, admiring her clothes. She had to admit that Shantell sure had some bad outfits. In the back of the closet, a long black leather trench coat caught her eye. Brenda pulled it from back, desperate to try it on.

Brenda attempted to put the coat on; she got one arm in the sleeve but when she tried to place the other arm in, it wouldn't go all the way down. Immediately she took off the coat to find out what was preventing her from putting her arm all the way in it. She never expected to find anything of significance. But she did.

Reaching her hand in the sleeve, Brenda pulled out three large zip-locked bags filled with several ounces of crack cocaine. Brenda stared at the boulders of crack in amazement. She had never seen this much cocaine in her life. Now Brenda was face to face with her nemesis, her weakness, her Achilles heel.

First Brenda valiantly fought the temptation. She immediately replaced all the drugs back in the sleeve, threw the coat on the bed and walked out of the room. Internally her mind waged a tug-of-war; it sent her body conflicting messages. It said, *Take a little a hit for old times sake.* Then it warned, *don't do it! You've come too far to throw it all away.*

Those old demons resurfaced and the addict in Brenda reared its ugly head. Drawn like a magnet, she walked back into the room and retrieved the drugs. Quickly but neatly she tore into one of the bags, pinching off a sizeable chunk of crack cocaine. Then she hung the coat back up in the closet, just as she had found it.

Momentarily, Brenda was overcome by a bad sensation; still, that didn't stop her from looking high and low for any household item she could use to assist in getting high. Nothing short of divine intervention was going to stop Brenda from smoking. She was about to re-enter those deep, dark waters of drug abuse. From this point on, there was no way back.

With one hand, Brenda placed the broken radio antenna to her lips, careful not to drop the small piece of crack cocaine that was lodged in the other end. Using her free hand, she slowly raised the lit cigarette lighter and set the crack cocaine ablaze. She inhaled deeply as the drug rushed into her lungs. Within seconds it took effect and she was overcome by a euphoric feeling. Brenda's heart began to beat wildly against her chest, and she exhaled a large cloud of crack smoke. If Brenda died right now, she would have died happy.

As Shantell drove to the party, she noticed a pair of bright strobe lights that seemed to the illuminate the sky. The closer she got to the party, the stronger they became. When Shantell pulled up to the Hyatt hotel, she discovered the source of the lights. This was one of the promoter's signature moves. Adolph rolled out the red carpet like this was a movie premiere. By the large amounts of people in line, one would have thought it was.

Shantell had a hard time finding parking. She had to park off the hotel premises and walk a short distance to the party.

The line to enter the party seemed to extend down the block and around the corner. Luckily, she had a VIP pass and after only a few moments, she breezed right pass the security checkpoint and gained entrance to the party.

From the moment she stepped in the place, Shantell felt like it was all eyes on her. She turned the heads of men and women alike. They all seemed to wonder the exact same thing" "Who was that?" Shantell caught all the stares of admiration, even the venomous stares of hate. She took them both in stride.

A lot of partygoers immediately assumed that Shantell was from out of town. Her face wasn't that recognizable with her Gucci shades on and also because she had just came of age to party with the older crowd.

Inside the party was like a large traffic jam. There was a sea of human bodies that didn't seem to budge. Shantell figured it would take her forever to find Mike in here. So instead of wasting her time looking for him, Shantell stepped into the ladies' room to make a call.

Mike was standing along the wall, politicking with some local thugs, when he got the call. He placed one finger in his ear then shouted, "Yo, what's up? You in here?"

Shantell replied, "Yeah, I just got here. I'm in the bathroom."

"Huh?" Mike hollered. "Speak up, I can't hear you!"

"I said I'm in the bathroom!" she barked. "Where you at?"

When Shantell raised her voice, she drew the ear of most of the women in the bathroom. They didn't think it was necessary to be talking that loud. They figured Shantell was trying to draw attention to herself to be seen. A few of them sucked their teeth loudly, to show their disapproval.

Shantell continued, "Yo, walk to the front and come get me."

"A'ight, stay right there. I'm on my way up there right now."

Mike aggressively weaved his way through the crowd. He bumped into dudes and brushed up on women. He found himself repeatedly saying, "Pardon me, fam. Excuse me, Miss." Never the less he made it to his destination.

Standing by the public pay phones, Mike whipped out his cell phone and dialed Shantell's number. "I'm out here! Yo, step outside the bathroom. I'm waitin' for you.".

"I'm comin' out right now!"

Mike directed his attention to the door. He was not prepared to see what he saw when it opened. Shantell sashayed out, looking good enough to eat. Mike had never seen her get her grown and sexy look on. To him, she had to be one of the best looking chicks in the entire party. Mike began lusting for her like he never had before.

"Goddamn!" he exclaimed. "Dat's crazy right there. All dat you?"

Shantell blushed. She loved all the attention Mike was now showering on her. It seemed like she had been waiting a long time for Mike to start feeling her like this. All this attention, however, would be short-lived.

"Hey, Mike," one woman said.

"Mike, you handsome motherfucker, you!" another woman commented.

Once it started it didn't seem to stop. Mike was a popular guy, but Shantell didn't know he was this popular. It seemed like chicks were just lining up to say hello, as if Mike was the mayor of Charlotte. She felt like all these outside diversions were taking away from her time. Still, she said nothing; she just stood to the side, looking real glamorous.

Mike could feel Shantell's tension from all the attention he was receiving. He was glad when he spotted a few of his other home boys from New York. They walked over and chilled for a while.

After exchanging daps and hugs, Mike turned and introduced Shantell to the crew.

"Yo, Shantell, this my man Sha. That's Rock. And that nigger over there is Dame."

"Hi," Shantell managed to say.

This introduction was done for two reasons: one, to appease Shantell. And two, to let Mike's people know that this was his bitch so if they should see her again, they knew what time it was: hands off.

As soon as Mike's crew left,, Adolph the promoter walked in followed by a large entourage. The first thing Shantell noticed about the group was that the guys were awfully big and tall. What she didn't know was that this was a group made up of professional athletes.

"Yo, Adolph!" Mike hollered. "C'mere."

Mike didn't really want anything; he was trying to impress Shantell. He wanted to show her he knew everybody and everybody knew him. He wanted to impress in her mind that he was a major figure in Charlotte and that she was lucky to be rolling with him.

As Mike and the promoter kicked it, his entourage lingered nearby. Coolly, Shantell glanced in their direction. She was careful not to look too long; she didn't want to be taken for a groupie. She didn't want to play herself or her man. Shantell

didn't get down like that. Even though Mike didn't deserve that
kind of respect, she gave it to him anyway.

Shantell thought to herself, *"There go that guy from the
draft, Ronald Wright. Damn, he tall!"*

She could have sworn a couple of times that she saw him
staring at her. Maybe he was and maybe he wasn't; Shantell
wasn't too sure. He might as well save his breath if he was
looking, because she was leaving here with Mike tonight.

Their conversation was over just as quick as it started.
Mike and Adolph parted ways. Shantell and Mike were alone for
the first time in a long time.

"Yo, you want something to drink?" Mike asked.

"Naw, I'm good."   "Look, it's kinda hot in here. Follow me outside for a minute."

Amazingly, there were still people outside hoping to gain
entrance to the party. That was pretty much a dead issue; the
Mecklenburg County Police Department was out there, and
they refused to let anyone else in. This party would go down as
one of the best ever seen, long after it was over.

Shantell followed Mike to the Hyatt car garage.

Before she knew it, they ended up in back seat of Mike's
Range Rover. Now it was time for her to handle her business.
Shantell performed oral sex on Mike like a pro. By now, she
knew what he liked and how he liked. When Mike climaxed,
she swallowed a mouthful of his semen while staring him
directly in his eye. She knew that would drive him wild, and it
did.

When they re-entered the party, courtesy of their bright
orange-colored VIP arm bands, Mike was in for quite a surprise.
Unbeknownst to him, his girlfriend, Tonya, and a group of her
friends were now in the party. Tonya stepped out from time to
time just to check on Mike. She wanted to make sure he was
being faithful. She had no concrete proof that he was a dog but
over the years she had heard her fair share of stories. She knew
everybody couldn't possibly be hating on him, as he claimed.

"Aye, yo, Mike, c'mere. Lemmie holla at you," Sha called out.

Shantell watched as Mike walked over to him. As soon as he was in arm's reach, Sha pulled Mike close and whispered something in his ear. Whatever Sha said, Shantell could see it changed Mike's whole attitude. A mean mug instantly masked his face.

"What's wrong?" she wondered aloud.

"Nuttin'!" Mike replied. "Just some bullshit. My people got a li'l drama wit' some niggers that owe him some dough. He don't like the fact that they partying' and ain't pay him."

Mike was lying through his teeth. He could never reveal his true reason for his sudden mood change. The fact that his main girl was in the club irritated the hell out of him. Immediately, he knew Tonya's girlfriends had put her up to coming out to the party, because Tonya knew that Mike didn't play that.

Now, all Mike knew was that he had to get rid of Shantell. If he ran into Tonya while he was with her, then there would be too much explaining to do. To his girlfriend, that is. She was the problem. Mike didn't give a damn about Shantell. He felt he could control her. Plus, she already knew the deal.

"Yo, look I need you to do something for me." Mike announced. "My man got something for me in the car. Get it and take it home for me. I'll be by tomorrow."

While Mike spoke, Shantell glanced over his shoulder and saw his man, Sha, hovering around. She wasn't happy that she had to leave to handle Mike's business, but she accepted the fact and followed orders like a good little soldier.

Just as Mike finished talking, out of nowhere his girlfriend Tonya appeared. She was a beautiful dark-skinned woman, a college-educated, sophisticated, professional type. Many people thought, including her friends, that she was too good for Mike. He didn't deserve her.

Tonya walked up to Mike, threw her arms around his neck and kissed him gently on the lips. She totally ignored

Shantell. Her actions spoke volumes, as if to say, "This is my man."

"Hey, babe. Where you been? I been looking all over for you."

When she spoke Mike smelled the liquor on her breath. Instantly he knew he had a problem. Tonya couldn't hold her liquor; when she got drunk, she tended to run off at the mouth. That was out of character for her.

"Yo, what you doin' here?" Mike questioned. "You been drinkin'?"

"What do you mean, what am I doin' here?" Tonya repeated. "What, I can't go out now? I stay in the house all the time, I needed a li'l break. My girl had an extra ticket, she asked me did I wanna go? So here I am. Anyway, who the hell is this?"

Who the hell is this? The comment echoed in Shantell's head.

This is the bitch that just sucked your man's dick. Shantell was burning up inside but she played cool. She didn't like anyone questioning someone else about her. Shantell was right there; she could speak for herself.

"Oh, that ain't nobody," Mike countered. "That's my man's girl. He standin' right there."

When Tonya glanced to her right and saw Sha, she felt so stupid.. Mike seized this opportunity to make his girlfriend feel bad.

"This the shit I'm talking' bout. You always think a nigga is doin' wrong. I'm tired of this shit!." Mike knew his comment would make Shantell mad, but he knew he could clean up that mess later. He was sure of it. Pretending to be mad, he stomped off in the opposite direction. Tonya ran right behind him, apologizing. Her buzz from the alcohol was completely gone.

❦

After leaving the party, Shantell's mind went blank. She didn't even remember taking the kilo of coke from Mike's friend. She jumped on the highway and sped home. She wanted to put an end to this disappointing night as quickly as possible.

The swirl of blue and white lights brought Shantell back to reality. Her heart sank. Suddenly, she remembered that she was dirty. She had a sneaker box full of drugs sitting in the passenger seat. Fear raced through her body. This was the moment she feared.

Shantell tried her best to remain calm. She took a few deep breaths but they didn't do her any good. She knew she had enough drugs in the car to get her a lot of time. Thoughts of her daughter flashed in her mind. How could she be so stupid to jeopardize herself and her child like this?

"Miss, license and registration please," the state trooper asked.

Complying with the officer, Shantell dug into her bag and retrieved her license. Then she reached into her glove compartment and grabbed her registration. She prayed that she didn't accidentally knock the box over because at that point the state trooper was watching her every move.

"Miss, is there any particular reason that you were speeding?" he asked. "Your vehicle was traveling 80 miles an hour in a 65 miles-per-hour zone."

Shantell thought it was best to play stupid. She didn't offer much of a defense.

"Officer, I didn't even realize I was goin' that fast. It didn't feel like I was goin' fast. At all"

"Okay, Miss. Just stay put. I'll be right back."

Shantell stared at the rearview mirror, watching the state trooper run her license for warrants. Shantell hoped like hell she didn't have any unpaid summonses or fines. That would give him probable cause to search the car, then it would be over for her.

Before she knew it, the state trooper returned to her car. He handed Shantell a speeding ticket then he gave her a lecture.

"Miss, please slow it down and be a little bit more mindful of the rate of speed you are traveling at. The speed laws are strictly enforced along this corridor of the highway. Over the years, we've had a lot of nasty accidents here. The traffic laws are enforced to protect all citizens."

Shantell took her ticket and reprimand in stride. She was glad she wasn't going to jail. She promised herself the first thing she was going to do when she got home was to kiss her daughter, Jordan. That close call with the law shook her up. For the rest of the way home she drove slow, like an old lady.

Chapter 11
The Fall Out

Weeks had passed since Mike played Shantell in front of Tonya, his real girlfriend. The very next day, Mike came over and cleaned up his mess as best as he could. He talked a good game, but in all reality it would never be the same. Shantell would only give herself to him because she needed to, not because she wanted to. Shantell may have reacted off pure emotions, but she wasn't stupid. She knew who paid the bills. Right now, she was just biding her time.

Shantell told herself repeatedly, *I'm not fuckin' wit' Mike like that no more.* Still, it was easier said than done. Her present good fortunes, and that of her daughter's, were currently tied to Mike's purse strings. She knew it but most importantly, he knew it too.

On one of her rare days alone, when her daughter was at daycare and her mother was supposedly looking for work, Mike paid her a surprise visit. He entered the apartment unannounced and barged into Shantell's room. It came as quite a shock to Shantell what Mike accused her of.

He announced, "Yo, I don't know what the fuck is goin' on 'round here, but somebody goin' tell me sumthin'!"

Shantell shot him a perplexed look.'

"Don't look at me like that. I ain't fuckin' stupid!"

"What!?" she blurted out.

Mike leaned back against the dresser, scanning Shantell's face for any hint of falsehood. The results of his personal lie detector test were inconclusive. Mike decided to stop beating around the bush and cut straight to the chase.

"Look, somebody's been tappin' the work. I don't know who it is, but everybody is suspect right now."

The reason why Shantell drew Mike's suspicion was because of the way he felt he embarrassed her at the party. Mike was a firm believer in the old saying, "Hell has no fury like a woman scorned." If it was one thing Mike knew about women, it was that they were sneaky characters. They tended to extract measures of revenge in some of the strangest ways. Maybe this was one of them.

Mike first discovered that someone in his organization was stealing when he started receiving a rash of complaints from his workers and customers to whom he was selling weight. He wasn't sure just how long the thievery had been going on, but he was trying to put an end to it. There was no telling what he was going to do when he identified the culprit.

What really angered Mike about the entire situation was that he thought he was more than generous with dividing the profits; so whoever was stealing from him was biting the hand that fed them. That was a no-no in his book. Mike didn't like anyone taking his kindness for a weakness. Examples had to be made.

"Listen, I ain't got no reason to steal from you," Shantell told him. "You been too good to me. I'm really kinda of fucked up that you would even think that of me. I been a lot things in my life, but I ain't never been no thief."

Shantell looked him straight in the eye and didn't flinch as she proclaimed her innocence. She was unapologetic in her speech and stood her ground. She refused to accept the blame for something she didn't do. She wasn't about to be anyone's scapegoat.

She continued, "Mike, if you think I stole from you, then you don't know me. If you don't know me, then ain't no sense in you fuckin' wit' me like that. You always trusted me before. I held a lot of fuckin' drugs for you before, and nothin' like this ever happened."

Though there was some truth in her words, Mike was too mad to really comprehend it. All he knew was that there was a weak link in the chain and he had to find out just who that was.

From here on out, Mike promised to monitor the situation more closely. Instead of chasing hoes, he vowed to get back on his job and stop leaving the success of his livelihood in someone else's hands. If this minor setback served any purpose, it put Mike back on point.

"Yo, here's what we gonna do, I'ma start weighin' the shit out in front of yo' face. Then, there can never be any discrepancies if shit comes up short."

Shantell nodded her head in agreement. At this point, she really didn't have too much choice in the matter. It was what it was now. Shantell was playing his game, so she had to abide by his rules. There was no doubt in her mind that the honeymoon was over.

For the rest of the day, Shantell was tense. Quietly she sat in her room, pondering the whole situation. All kinds of scenarios played themselves out in her head. Maybe Mike was just trying to cut her off and he needed a reason, so he made this story up so he could hide his true intentions. As she played devil's advocate, suddenly it hit her. Brenda.

Shantell kicked herself for not thinking of this earlier. That explained everything. Who else could have possibly had access to the drugs? And why had this suddenly happened? Somehow, her mother must have found Mike's stash. This explained her extended periods away from the house, under the pretense of job hunting. Her mother was getting high again.

A sad thought ran through her mind: "Once a junkie always a junkie."

When Jordan arrived home from daycare, Shantell interrogated her daughter. She used her like the Army would use any spy and she pumped the child for information.

"Jordan, does Grandma be in my room while I'm gone?" She gently asked.

Jordan replied, "Yeah, sometimes. She be tryin' on your clothes, Mommy."

Oh, yeah? Shantell mused. *So it is true.* "What else does she do when I'm not here?"

"Grandma takes a real long time in the bathroom."

"And what else?" Shantell insisted.

"I don't know?" Jordan said.

Shantell decided against continuing with her line of questioning. Her daughter had said a mouthful. If this was court, then Brenda just got convicted on the word of a Five year old.

This was all Shantell needed to invade her mother's privacy. She began to search the apartment, concentrating her search on her mother's room and the bathroom.

In Brenda's suitcase she found a smoke-blackened stem from a free base pipe, wrapped up in old clothes. In the bathroom underneath the sink, she found crack cocaine-laden razor blades. Suddenly the pieces of the puzzle all fell in place.

Without Brenda present all the physical evidence was like knowing someone committed murder, without finding the body. Shantell couldn't wait for her mother to come through that front door. She was going to give her an earful.

Shantell's expected confrontation with her mother would have to wait a little longer. Brenda was a no-show that night and the following day. On the third day she finally showed her face; luckily for Shantell, her daughter was in daycare. Jordan didn't need to see or hear them going at it. This was grown folk's business.

Silently, Brenda opened the door and eased her way into the apartment. Like a cat burglar, she maneuvered her way towards Shantell's room. After listening at the door for a few seconds, Brenda worked up the nerve to go in.

Brenda knew Shantell's schedule like the back of her hand. Once she saw her daughter onto the school bus, she usually went back to sleep. Brenda counted on this to be the case today.

The low, steady squeak of her bedroom door alerted Shantell to Brenda's presence. Not for one moment did she believe it was anyone else. If it was, she was in trouble. Shantell decided to take her chances. She lay in the bed motionless, lying on her side, with her back toward the door, Shantell pretended to be fast asleep. She even added some fake snoring for good measure.

Brenda bit on the fake. She slithered her way further and further into the room. She was at the point now where there was no turning back. There was no way Brenda was leaving this room without her medicine. The closer she got, the more impatient she became. That led to Brenda making more noise. Just as she was about to open the closet door, Shantell silently rose from her bed.

"What the fuck you think you doin? Huh?"

Brenda almost pissed in her pants. She clutched her shirt in surprise. She was scared, then the shame and embarrassment began to set in. She was caught. Her daughter knew she was getting high again.

Shantell continued, "I caught yo' ass, didn't I?"

This was when Brenda's old street, crack head con game kicked in. Now it was a matter of self–preservation. She needed to save herself so she told a lie, because the truth was unaccept-able. Telling Shantell the truth now would get Brenda a one-way ticket out of her apartment, and maybe her life, for good.

"What you talking about?" Brenda blurted out. "I was just going in your closet to borrow one of your jackets. I'm sorry for not asking you first. Is that what you so mad about?"

"Who the fuck you think you lying to?" Shantell snapped. "You think I'm stupid? How long you thought you was gonna get away wit' this? Huh? Bitch, you gettin' high again!"

"What? What you talking about? I been clean for almost a year, Brenda stated. "I just came in here to borrow a jacket."

Shantell didn't bother to reply. She merely reached over into her nightstand and pulled out a clear zip-locked bag filled with drug paraphernalia. This was proof that her mother wasn't as clean as she claimed.

"Bitch, does this look familiar?"

In a flash, Shantell threw the paraphernalia at her mother. Fortunately for Brenda, the contents of the bag weren't heavy enough to travel that far through the air. The bag landed harmlessly by the end of the bed. But Shantell wasn't through with her yet. She jumped off the bed in a threatening manner she walked over to her mother. Shantell's teeth were clenched and her fists were balled up tight, as if she was ready to fight.

For a moment, Brenda didn't even recognize her daughter. She didn't know who this madwoman was or what she was capable of doing. Brenda sensed danger, so she began backpedaling out of the room.

"You crack head bitch!" Shantell spat. "I let you into my fuckin' house. Take you back into my life, even when you didn't deserve it. You lived for months in my house, rent-free. And this is how you repay me!"

There was nothing between Brenda and Shantell but air and Brenda's fear. Finally, Shantell cornered her in the hallway.

As bad as Shantell wanted to hit Brenda, she couldn't bring herself to do it. Instead she just pointed her finger in her mother's face to emphasize her point as she talked loudly.

"This how you do me, huh? You disrespected my house and my daughter by smokin' crack in the bathroom. And the bad thang is, you stealin' shit, that don't even belong to me. Suppose some nigga's woulda came in here and killed me and Jordan over some shit that you did? Huh?"

Brenda never even looked at the situation like that. She was too busy getting high to even care. She never thought about what the consequence of her actions would have on her family.

Shantell continued. "You would think that you wouldn't play me like that. You know I was kind enough to reach out to you after all the shit you done. I created a space for you to live comfortably. That room you was sleepin' in, that ain't yo' room. That's my daughter's room. I got her sleepin' with me. For what? You know what? I'm fuckin' through with you. Pack yo' shit and get the fuck outta my house."

Brenda never had a chance to get a word in edgewise. Shantell had given her the business. She didn't care what her mother had to say. Her mind was made up, days ago; she knew she was putting her mother out. Still, Shantell didn't feel good about the manner in which they were parting ways.

Right now she did not care to admit it, but despite everything that happened she still had love for her mother. She had a heart; filled with emotions buried deep down inside; and now that heart was hurting. Still, she refused to let her mother see that side of her. She refused to expose her pain, yet she couldn't stand the thought of being without her mother again. Somehow through this misery that had become her life, Shantell had already been through this, not once but now twice. It didn't hurt any less the second time around.

With her mother gone, Shantell felt like now it was really time to get herself together, to get her life in order. She began to focus on the shape of her future, on her daughter.

She knew it was time to get back on her grind. So it was back to the club.

Chapter 12
How Playas Play

"Way to move your feet! Good rotation," The coach yelled. "That's what I'm talking about DEFENSE. Defense wins championships."

A smile spread over the coach's face. Finally, he was starting to see the fruits of the team's hard labor. It seemed like the team was beginning to buy into his defense-oriented system. On the defensive end they were beginning to play like one cohesive unit, with everyone defending for the entire ninety feet.

Leading the charge was the energetic rookie, Ronald Wright. He ran through the scrimmage without breaking a sweat. He was making it hard for the coach to keep him off the court. If the coach wasn't so old-fashioned in that he didn't start rookies, then maybe Ronald would have been a starter when the NBA season kicked off a few days from now. Lord knows he deserved it.

"Gather 'round," the coach suggested.

The players towered over him as they put their arms into a huddle to show team unity.

The coach continued, "Defense on three. One, two, three."

"Defense!" the team roared in unison.

When the whistle blew it signaled more than the end of the scrimmage; It signaled the end of practice and training camp. Some Charlotte Bobcat players couldn't have been more relieved. Not Ronald Wright;, he wished they had practice every day. He was in the best shape of his life.

Immediately after the draft, Ronald hired a personal trainer and moved to Charlotte. The world-renowned fitness guru had trained some of most elite athletes in the world. When it came to working out, he was a no pain, no gain type. His grueling drills pushed Ronald to his limit, testing his tolerance for pain. Over summer he had packed on ten pounds of muscle. He had a chiseled body and rock–hard, washboard abs to for all his hard work. Not that Ronald was in bad shape before, but now he was more than ready to face the dreaded rookie wall, the rigors of the long NBA season.

The veteran NBA players had already begun to disperse but a group of five or so younger players lingered on the court. This was the nucleus of the Bobcat youth movement. These players talked in hushed tones, careful to keep anyone out of their circle, out of their business. When Ronald passed by, gulping down the last of his Gatorade, they called him over.

"Yo, Ron," someone called out. "C'mere real quick."

Slowly Ronald headed towards the group. He wondered just what this was all about. What did they want with him? Ronald was somewhat of a loner on the team. He didn't come to the NBA to make friends. He came to leave a legacy as one of the best players to ever lace up a pair of sneakers.

He knew most of the players didn't like him and vice versa. They were from two different worlds. He was from the suburbs, middle class, and many of them were from the mean streets of the inner city. Had it not been for the game of basketball, then more than likely their paths would never have crossed. It was somewhat of a culture clash for all parties involved.

Still, they all had to admit that Ronald Wright had game. He spoke the universal language of basketball fluently. Those were the two things they all had in common: basketball and youth.

"What's up, fellas?" Ronald spoke. "What's going on?"

"Listen, its Eric's birthday today," one player began. "A group of us were gettin' together a li'l later tonite to celebrate. We was thinkin', maybe you wanna chill wit' us tonight?"

"Sorry fellas, I don't," he stated. "Anyway, I have to get some rest."

The player responded, "C'mon man don't be like that. Don't be a party pooper. Where's yo' team spirit? How we gonna build chemistry and camaraderie, if you over there and we over here? It's just one night, man. I promise, you can leave early."

Ronald had to admit, they had a point. He had worked like a dog all summer; he deserved a little break. He thought to himself, *What better way to get to know your teammates?*

"You partied with us last time," another player interjected.

"Alright, count me in," Ronald stated.

"That's what's up!" someone commented. "It's goin' to be on tonight."

After accepting their invitation, Ronald headed for the locker room. He was unsure of just what to expect out of his teammates tonight, but he would bet his last dollar it was going to be fun.

−❧❧−

Every time Shantell dropped Jordan off at the babysitter, she felt real bad. It was almost as if she was betraying her daughter. Jordan left her mother with images of her kicking, screaming and crying her eyes out. Usually that would bring Shantell to tears. She hated to leave her daughter with virtual strangers, but she had no choice. After that incident with Mike, she was determined to liberate herself financially. She promised herself she would never again be at his mercy.

Tonight it was business as usual, except Shantell wouldn't be performing at the club. She lucked up and got invited by another stripper, Champagne, with whom she was friendly, to a private party. Just by the location of the party, Shantell knew that this wasn't going be your typical stripper affair.

Shantell and a few other strippers met up at Ballantyne Resort, located in the prestigious neighborhood of South Charlotte. The girls were told to be tastefully dressed, nothing scandalous or revealing, when entering the hotel. This was so as not to draw the suspicions of management, who had no idea that their establishment was being used for this purpose.

"Damn, this hotel real nice," one stripper gushed. "Must cost these niggers an arm and a leg to rent a room."

The identity of the occupants of the suite was kept a secret. Only one person actually knew who was up in the room, and Champagne wasn't saying. She knew if the word got out around the club, every stripper and their mother would want to come. She knew everything wasn't for everybody. She selected the prettiest girls with the nicest bodies and good character. But more importantly, they had to be down for whatever. It was on her to show these dudes a good time. If everything worked out, then she knew that they would be hollering at her again, for sure.

"Don't worry they can afford it," Champagne assured them.

"That's all a bitch like me needed to hear. Ya heard!" another stripper commented.

As they entered the resort, the sudden appearance of four sexy African American females caught the desk person's eye. He stopped them immediately.

"Good evening, ladies. Welcome to the Ballantyne Resort. Here, we like to think of it as heaven on earth," he greeted them. "How can I help you?"

Champagne replied, "Yes. We're here to see a gentleman in suite 310. I believe his name is Roger Thornton."

Quickly, the desk person punched the name into the computer to verify the guest's stay at the resort. Once everything checked out, he directed the ladies to the elevator.

"Take a left at the end of this corridor and the elevators will be on your immediate right. Have a nice night, ladies."

"Thank you, sir," Champagne replied.

The small entourage strutted down the hall, marveling at all the nice fixtures in the lobby. The luxurious getaway was much to their liking. They soaked it all up with their eyes; most knew that they had never been to a place this nice before and probably wouldn't again. This hotel gave luxury a whole new meaning.

As the elevator rose to the designated floor, the more impatient Shantell became. She was getting tired of all this cloak-and-dagger stuff. She couldn't wait to see just who these big timers were. She figured they were in the music industry, probably a rapper and his homeboys. But there was one thing for certain: there was some money in that suite.

The elevators doors opened silently and the girls exited all at once. Since this was Champagne's hook up, naturally she led the way, followed by Juicy, Shantell and Delicious. After knocking softly on the door, they waited for entrance. From the outside, they heard a short burst of laughter.

Suddenly, the door flew open. All the women looked up. Shantell thought, *Damn, this nigger's tall!*

"Damn, y'all lookin' good as a motherfucker," the player remarked. "Don't just stand there; come in."

One by one, the ladies entered the Presidential Suite. Inside, they were greeted by more tall men. Shantell didn't know if the other girls already recognized them or not, but she already knew who these dudes were: members of the Charlotte Bobcats.

It didn't take long for the other strippers to catch on. From her vantage point, Shantell could see them suddenly starting to change. They began to act like a bunch of groupies, finger pointing and getting loud.

"Oh, I want that one right over there," Juicy shouted.

Delicious replied, "You can have that one, but I got that big, black nigger sittin' right there on the couch.

From that point on Shantell knew exactly how it was going down. It was every woman for herself. It seemed like money turned these strippers into mercenaries, and mercenaries into savages. Sad part about it was, there was more than enough money to go around.

When the girls walked in, it was like a soul train line. For a moment, all eyes were transfixed on them. In their minds, the guys did the same thing: they chose which one they wanted; they just didn't openly express it. One by one the players walked over and introduced themselves. The two groups became one as everybody began to socialize.

Shantell took the time to soak up her surroundings. The Presidential Suite was humongous. It was larger than all of the girls' apartments. There was a sunken living room with a nice tan leather sectional couch. Art work seemed to be hanging from every wall. Both of the 42-inch plasma televisions were tuned to ESPN's *Sports Center*. There was a fully stocked bar in the corner. All the amenities of home could be found here.

"Champagne, lemmie holla at you for a minute," one of the players said.

Shantell watched intently as the player and Champagne talked. She noticed that he inconspicuously slipped her a wad of money. The other girls might have missed it, but she sure didn't. Shantell had been promised three hundred dollars just for coming and doing her thing. By the end of the night she aimed to collect it, too.

As she scanned the room Shantell silently began to identify each player. She noticed one player off to himself, in the distance. His eyes were glued to the television. He seemed very interested in the results of a golf tournament. The longer Shantell stared at him, the more familiar his face became.

Oh, shit! That's the dude from the draft. Ronald Wright, she thought to herself.

Once again their paths had intersected; first it was the party at the Hyatt, and now here. She wondered if he would recognize her, not that she had done anything to make herself memorable. She thought he probably wouldn't. She wondered how many girls threw themselves at him daily.

"C'mon, y'all, let's go get changed," Champagne commanded.

Obediently the girls followed the order. They all entered an oversized bedroom and began changing from their street clothes to their work outfits. Digging in their bags, each girl pulled out sexy stripper outfits with stilettos to match. Shantell opted to just wear a thong and go topless; even though she brought a few outfits herself, in the end she decided to keep it simple.

When they re-entered the room, Shantell felt a nervous energy in the air. The show was about to begin and so was the feeding frenzy. These were top-notch athletes with huge sexual appetites. They were used to the best of the best and this was no different; the freakier the better.

"Where the birthday boy at?" Delicious shouted.

"Right here!" The group said in unison.

The atmosphere inside the suite began to resemble a college fraternity house. There were lots of imitation dog barks and loud cheering going on, mainly boys being boys.

While the girls were in the bedroom, the players had re-arranged the furniture, creating more room. Quickly, everyone gathered in the living room; it was show time. Delicious grabbed the birthday boy's hand and took him over to the couch and gave him an awesome lap dance. That was just for starters. When that was done, she undid his pants and gave him a blowjob right in front of everybody.

Ronald Wright blended safely into the background. He was just as shocked as he was stimulated. He was enjoying the proceedings. He had a wild side in him that he suppressed. He didn't put his business in the street like this. He was more of a closet freak.

Meanwhile, Juicy and Champagne began putting on their own show. Using a large black strap-on dildo, the two strippers began servicing each other. The sight of two women having sex aroused every man in the room. There wasn't a soft penis in the suite.

The birthday celebration became the ultimate freak-off. Everybody seemed to be oblivious to each other's doings; they were too busy doing the damn thing. Condoms and articles of clothing littered the room.

Shantell thought to herself, *this bitch going all out!*

By this time, everybody had chosen their partners. The most aggressive strippers picked the players who were bejeweled with expensive diamond-encrusted wristwatches and expensive platinum chains. As fate would have it, this paired Shantell with Ronald.

"Hey, Big Man, what's up wit' you? You participatin' or just watchin'?" Shantell asked him. "What you tryin' to do?"

Ronald was caught off guard by Shantell's straightforwardness. It caused him to blush. He had never in his life been propositioned like this. His mother did a good job of sheltering her son away from the scandalous groupies, so far.

Right away, Shantell could see that he was the shy type. Though he may have been big physically, he still was a kid. He was a man-child. She could see he was more than a little bashful. The average guy would have been all over her by now, so Shantell knew that if she didn't make the first move, then nothing was happening. She'd be there all day waiting on him. Ronald represented a dollar sign to her. The act of sex was just a way to feed her daughter.

Seizing the moment, Shantell grabbed his hand and led him away from this orgy. Suddenly they found themselves in the bedroom. Behind closed doors, it was a different story. Ronald suddenly underwent a drastic transformation, sort of like Dr. Jekyll and Mr. Hyde. He was all over Shantell, pulling her close to him. His big hands engulfed her butt cheeks. He palmed her butt and breasts as if they were basketballs.

No words needed to be exchanged between the two. There was no time for talk only action. Breaking loose from his grip, Shantell went south on Ronald. She knew her fellatio was the bomb, so she got on her knees and began to handle her business. When Shantell opened his zipper and removed Ronald's penis, she was expecting him to be well hung. Boy was she in for a surprise. Ronald was not holding at all. To say he had an average-sized penis might have been an overstatement.

Judging by the size of his hands and his big feet, one would have thought that Ronald would be a monster downstairs. Ronald dispelled that old rumor by which women usually used to measure the size of a man's manhood. Now Shantell knew for sure that this didn't apply to everybody.

Wow! Shantell thought to herself. *That's it, huh?*

Shantell felt bad for him. Still, she performed like her usual self. She took him into her mouth and easily deep-throated him.

From time to time, she glanced upward as she bobbed her head. She could see Ronald was enjoying her services. His eyes were shut tight and his hand rested atop Shantell's head, assisting her with the rhythm.

Without saying a word, Ronald pushed her away. Shantell knew he was about to climax so she locked her mouth on him like a pit bull and wouldn't let go. Literally he had to pry her mouth off him. Ronald didn't want to end the fun just yet. To him, Shantell was so sexy, that he wanted to see how it felt to be inside her.

"Damn, girl! What you tryin' to do to me?" he asked.

"I want you! Fuck me!" Shantell said seductively. "I wanna feel you inside me."

At that point Ronald came to his senses; he knew he couldn't have unprotected sexual intercourse with her. He wasn't really worried about catching a disease; he was more worried about getting someone pregnant. Having a baby out of wedlock was bad for his wholesome image. Besides that, he knew his mother would kill him.

Luckily, he had a condom in his back pocket. One of the guys had passed them out just before the strippers had arrived. At the time, he wondered when he would put it to use; now he knew. Ronald quickly produced the contraceptive and with his teeth, he tore into the protective wrapping. Now he was in business.

Deciding against having sex with his clothes on, Ronald disrobed. He was an amazing physical specimen. Ronald's body was in tip-top shape. He had muscles on top of muscles and low body fat. Shantell was thoroughly impressed.

As they headed to the bed, silently Shantell hoped that size didn't matter. She hoped that Ronald could work his thing. She ran across a lot of dudes that were holding but couldn't please her. But if worse came to worst, she planned on faking it. It would be her little secret, and he would never know.

Shantell crawled onto the bed and got into the doggy position, giving Ronald a good view of her round butt. Ronald couldn't help himself; he bent over and began licking her anus. The move took Shantell by surprise; still she enjoyed it.

When Ronald inserted his penis into her vagina, it was just as she suspected; he didn't do anything for her. He thrust his hips hard and fast, and his pelvis smacked Shantell's butt cheeks. Just watching her behind jiggle excited Ronald to the point he couldn't contain himself any more. Suddenly, he withdrew his penis from Shantell's vagina as he climaxed. He knew condoms weren't foolproof, so it was better to be safe than sorry.

"Yo, Ron, you alright in there?" someone yelled through the door.

Ronald lay motionless and drained, at the end of the bed. He was just savoring the moment. He replied, "Yeah, I'm cool! I'm coming out in a minute."

"Take yo' time!" The voice said.

When Ronald glanced down at his Rolex wristwatch, he realized it was getting late. He better start getting on his way before his mother started calling. If Ronald wasn't home by a certain time, she tended to fear for his safety.

Simultaneously, Shantell and Ronald began to get dressed. As he pulled on his pants, Ronald reached into his pocket and gave her a handful of large bills.

"Thanks," she said.

"No, thank you. The pleasure was all mines. Listen, do you mind if we exchange numbers? I would like to keep in contact with you. See you again, sometimes. I think you're beautiful."

Without hesitation, Shantell rattled off her number to him. She viewed him as a meal ticket. This was more than a come up; messing with Ronald would be like hitting the Power ball for a chick from the hood.

To her, it didn't matter if he didn't have that "good dick." From past experience she knew that 'good dick' didn't pay the rent, so she was more than willing to overlook his sexual shortcomings. She thought she could train a dick to meet her sexual needs, even one as little as Ronald's.

CHAPTER 13

EVERYBODY LOVES A STAR

If this is a dream, then please, God, don't wake me! Shantell thought to herself.

Ever since she met Ronald Wright, she seemed to be enjoying a magical carpet ride. Often she wondered when it would end. She wondered when would her prince turn into a frog. Shantell knew her luck didn't run like that. She felt like good things just didn't happen to her. It was as if she were cursed.

It wasn't like anything was wrong either. Her sexual relationship with Ronald had turned into a courtship of sorts in only a few short months. Somehow Shantell had managed to parlay their no-strings-attached, initial sexual encounter into something more meaningful. So everything was fine; she just found it strange that everything in her life was going so right, all of a sudden.

Suddenly there was a light at the end of the tunnel. Before that, those lights were the headlights of an oncoming train, named Misery that collided often with Shantell on the path of life. The future appeared to be bright for a change. But somehow, Shantell had a hard time believing it.

This was one of the most carefree times of her life. The only thing Shantell really worried about was getting rid of Mike. She was growing wary of his continued involvement in the drug game. She knew that one mistake by him, and either the police raiding her house or the stick-up boys kicking in her door, could bring her whole world crashing down.

Once she met Ronald, Shantell knew it was basically over for her and Mike. She planned on cutting him off all the way around the board. She was going to get her key back from him and hand him back his drugs. She really thought it would be that easy, but that remained to be seen.

Shantell saw no future with Mike; he was stop gap, temporary. After all, he was a drug dealer. She knew one of three fates usually befell a drug dealer: either they got locked up, arrested or got killed. Only a few were fortunate enough to get out of the game unscathed.

Right now, Mike was just an afterthought. She would deal with him later. Currently her mind was focused on her date with Ronald tonight.

The TGI Friday's restaurant, located on West Harris Boulevard, was packed to capacity. It was always like this every Friday. In Charlotte, it was the place to see and be seen. The restaurant was more than an eatery; it was more like a gathering spot, a fashion show and a social club, all rolled up into one.

When Ronald's black BMW 650i coupe pulled into the parking lot of TGIF, it seemed like heads suddenly turned and all conversations ceased. The expensive European sedan attracted lots of attention for both driver and passenger. The car was immaculately detailed, the body was waxed, and the tires shined, courtesy of a healthy coat of Armor All. Ronald opted to keep the car plain. Even without the fancy rims, tinted windows and other after-market accessories, the car still looked good. Ronald wasn't a flashy type of guy; he knew the value of money and to him, it made no sense to do anything to a car when the value of it depreciates as soon as you roll it off the lot.

A small crowd of patrons had gathered outside the restaurant's main entrance. Ronald excused himself and weaved his way through the crowd as he made his way to the hostess.

"Excuse me, Miss. How long is the wait?" he asked.

"It depends on how many people are in your party, sir," She retorted.

"Just two."

"Okay, the wait for a table is approximately a half hour to 45 minutes. Would you like to be placed on our waiting list?"

"Yes."

"Last name, sir?"

"Wright."

The hostess then handed him a dark, drink coaster-shaped pager. Ronald turned and walked back outside to his date. Suddenly Ronald found it difficult to maneuver his way out of the restaurant. People had begun to notice who he was. Fans and groupies alike showered him with accolades and compliments.

"Good game, man!" one person shouted. "That move you put of Kobe was crazy."

"Damn, that nigger is fine," a woman called out.

Ronald smiled, shook hands, and even signed a few autographs, for as many people as possible. This was a rare moment for him out in the public eye. He was just starting to see just how much professional athletes were adored in Charlotte.

Finally he made his way back to Shantell. He almost expected her to be mad for taking so long. It surprised him that she wasn't upset at all.

"Sorry I took so long, but it got kind of crazy in there for a minute." you aren't upset with me, are you?"

"Why would I be?" Shantell countered. "I know this comes wit' the territory. It's a part of yo' job."

Ronald broke out into a huge grin. He was glad that Shantell understood. In college, he had lost numerous girlfriends over the exact same thing. One thing that Ronald observed about many females that he dealt with in the past was that when it came time to demonstrating their understanding, they couldn't. Most couldn't handle all the attention that females fans gave him; Shantell, on the other hand, took it like a champ.

"I'm glad you think like that. You know what Shantell? I'm starting to like you more and more each day."

His comment made Shantell laugh lightly. She appreciated the compliment.

While they waited, the couple made small talk to kill the time. They began to take note of all the people pointing and staring in their direction. They heard all the murmurs and whispers from overexcited fans. It became an inside joke as they silently counted all the people.

"Got one behind you," Shantell would whisper.

"Incoming!" Ronald spoke softly. "I see another one to your right."

Outside the restaurant, Ronald and Shantell continued to laugh and joke. Before long their pager began to buzz and soon after they heard Ronald's last name being announced over the intercom system.

"Wright, party of two. That's Wright, party of two. Your table is now ready." the hostess announced.

By now the line to enter the restaurant had slowly diminished; still Ronald and Shantell had to run the gauntlet of well-wishers. They moved through the sea of people as quickly as possible, following the hostess they were seated in a dark booth in the back.

Though Charlotte may have been a big city, it had a small-town feel to it. Everybody knew everybody and sometimes everybody tended to be all up in your business. Shantell drew just as many stares as Ronald did. If she thought that she was some anonymous chick on his arm, she was wrong.

There were people in the restaurant who knew Shantell very well. Some knew her from the neighborhood or school, while many others knew her from the strip club. There were no secrets in Charlotte; a lot of people knew Shantell's background. Many of them wondered how she had come up on an NBA player.

From the outside looking in, it was hard for a lot of females in attendance to believe that Shantell had anything on them. The consensus in the restaurant was that she was damaged goods. They didn't believe that she was the better woman or even the right woman, for that matter, for Ronald Wright. For outsiders, it was much easier to label her a whore.

Unbeknownst to Shantell, sprinkled in with the local haters were a few of Mike's friends. People that knew of her, but whom she didn't even know. Immediately they jumped on their cellular phones to deliver the bad news to Mike. Some of the callers actually wanted to joke Mike about it. But for Mike, it wouldn't be a laughing matter.

Whether Shantell knew it or not, stepping out in public with another guy was a no-no. Even though Mike had a girl at home, Shantell was seen as being his girl too, although she was his side chick. This was total disrespect.

While Mike's cellular phone was being blown up with messages. Shantell and Ronald settled into their booth and ordered their meal. There was an awkward moment of silence as they quietly admired each other. For Shantell, it was now or never. It was time for her to lay her cards on the table and let the chips fall where they may. All she knew was that there was no way she was going to let this opportunity slip away from her.

"Listen, we been seein' a lotta each other lately," she admitted. "I know it started out as a fuck thing. But I'm startin' to catch feelings for you. I know this is still young, but I wanted you to know everything about me. I wanted to be the first to tell you."

Ronald listened intently while Shantell ran down her life story. He wore the stern look of a poker player on his face. There was no way for her to detect any emotion either way. When the food was served, they completely ignored it. Shantell continued to talk and Ronald opted to listen.

It was like therapy for Shantell to recount the trial and tribulations of her life. Facing adversity had molded Shantell. It had made her stronger and tougher. It had made her a woman. There was an old saying that went, 'struggle builds character.' This was definitely the case with her.

The entire time she spoke, Ronald didn't interrupt her once. He let her get all of the ill feelings she had pinned up inside her, out into the open. Shantell appreciated his patience; sometimes all she needed was a shoulder to cry on. Sometimes all she needed was to be able to tell the truth and not have to worry about being judged for her straightforwardness. Over the years a lot of people had heard her story, but he was the only one who really listened.

"Wow!" He sighed. "I can't believe all that happened to you. There are some very sick people in this world."

Ronald may not have shown it, but initially he was taken aback by the story. He was from a different world, and things like this didn't happen in his world. Shantell's story was the kind he read about in the newspaper. Usually only the perpetrator's picture was shown, never the victim. Now he had a face to attach to the crime.

If Shantell thought that her story would run Ronald away, she was sadly mistaken. He was a very compassionate human being. Instead of taking pity on her, as many people did, he sympathized with her. His heart went out to her. He was touched that she picked him to share her story with. It endeared her to him.

To Ronald, life wasn't all about what happened to a person during its course but how that person reacted to it. Shantell had rolled with life's punches. She was a survivor and he respected that. She could have easily given up on life, and taken her own life along time ago but she was still here. She was still alive, living to fight another day. That boded well with his competitive spirit. Ronald didn't like a weak woman.

Although Shantell had poured out her heart to him, telling him everything about her life, the paternity issue surrounding her daughter, her mother's on and off again drug habit and her brutal rape; she wisely omitted the presence of Mike in her life. She didn't think that Ronald was that understanding. She knew that men were easily threatened by other men. She knew that one man couldn't stand the fact that another might be sleeping with his woman. That thought alone could get a woman killed. Besides that, in her mind, she and Mike were a done deal.

Even in a restaurant full of people, Shantell and Ronald felt alone. For a brief moment they were the only ones that existed. Leave it to an overzealous fan to bring them back to reality.

"Oh, my God!" the woman cried. "It's Ronald Wright! My son loves you. He's your biggest fan. He wears the same number as you and everything. Could you please be so kind and sign an autograph for him?"

The woman thrust a pen and paper in his face. She waited patiently for him to accept her request as if it were a given. She stood there as if she knew he was going to sign an autograph to her son, like he had to.

This was the part of his celebrity that Ronald detested. He couldn't even enjoy his meal in peace, like normal people do. People could be so rude at times. They imposed on him at the wrong times. The situation was a catch-22. He was damned if he didn't and damned if he did. Ronald was caught up in trying to please everybody. He hadn't realized yet, that he never would.

What's you son's name, ma'am?" he inquired.

"Oh?" She sighed. "David Martin. And could you write something nice and inspirational? He really looks up to you."

Shantell rolled her eyes and sucked her teeth in response to her demands. She was ready to tell the woman off but she didn't, only because it would look bad on Ronald, especially if the press got hold of the story. It was for that reason alone that she bit her tongue.

After he finished signing that autograph, the woman shoved another piece of paper in his face. She claimed this one was for her nephew. She was really testing his patience right now. Still, Ronald never let on. He remained cool and calm; once again doing as he was told.

Ronald had started something. Before he knew it, his date turned into an autograph session. Quickly a line had formed from the bar to his table. People were taking pictures of him with camera phones. It got real crazy inside the restaurant and pretty soon, Ronald and Shantell had to leave. He was as nice as could be while exiting the restaurant. Still, he heard more than his fair share of criticism.

Someone yelled, "Oh, that's messed up, you signed hers and you didn't sign mine!"

"You ain't all that, anyway!" another person stated.

"I ain't neva goin' to another Bobcats game," someone else claimed.

Together Ronald and Shantell jumped in his car and quickly fled the scene. He didn't like the vibe inside the restaurant. It was situations like this that had him thinking about getting bodyguards. That way he could let his security play the role of the bad guy.

"Yo, I don't know how you put up wit' that shit, day in and day out," Shantell stated. "You see how ignorant people can get?"

"You don't have to tell me, I already know. It's something I gotta deal with. They pay me well to do it."

"I heard that. But me, personally, I couldn't have kept my cool. Everyday ain't a good day for me! Sometimes I wake up on the wrong side of the bed."

He retorted, "Well, I can't afford to wake up on the wrong side of the bed."

In silence Ronald drove towards Shantell's apartment complex. It was clear that he was drained from all the excitement. Right then, he just wanted some sleep. He wanted to forget about that madhouse known as TGI Friday's.

"Guess what?"

"What?"

"My mother wants to me you. I told her about you," Ronald admitted.

"Why?"

"My mother wanted to know where I was going to-night. So I told her I was going on a date with Shantell Bryant."

"Damn, you told her my whole name, huh?"

"Sure did," he nonchalantly replied.

Shantell had long ago suspected that Ronald was a little momma's boy. Now she knew.

"Alright, whatever! Just let me know when she wanna meet me, and we'll meet." Inwardly Shantell smiled to herself. This was big. She knew that guys in general, especially guys of Ronald Wright's caliber, didn't just take any old body to meet their parents. So to her, that was a good sign.

Shantell's mind raced from the time Ronald told her, till the time she went to sleep that night. She wondered what Ronald's mother was like. She hoped the woman like her. If she didn't, Shantell felt she didn't stand a chance with Ronald.

❧

The platinum Range Rover whipped into TGI Friday's parking lot. Mike hopped out of his car and walked swiftly towards the entrance. He hoped he was in time to catch Shantell in the restaurant with the ball player. Prior to him coming there, he had turned his phone off. He was spending some quality time with his lady at home. But every so often he would check his cellular phone for messages. When he got the word about Shantell, he quickly got dressed and flew to the restaurant. To be honest, Mike's pride was hurt. He couldn't believe that she would disrespect him like that. He had to see it for himself.

When Mike walked through the door, he didn't really pay attention to anyone. His mind was focused on Shantell. When he did look in different directions all he saw was a bunch of chicks he had already had.

"Yo, Mike!" came a voice from the bar area. "C'mere!"

When Mike got over there the guy could see he wasn't in a joking mood, but he didn't care. Mike had, on more than one occasion, clowned him about women that he perceived as playing him. Now he was just returning the favor.

"Is that yo' chick, why she all on his dick…is that yo' chick?" He mocked a popular rap song by Jay-Z. "Yo, son, you just missed her. She was all up in here wit' this tall, basketball-playin' muthafucka…ummm, ummm, what's his name… Ronald sumthin.' Oh yeah, that rookie nigger Ronald Wright."

The man's words stung Mike; he heard all he needed to know. Inside his gut there was this sickening feeling of jealousy. Still, he didn't want to give off the appearance that he really cared for some hoe. The fact that he was there was admission enough. Mike resisted the urge to leaving the restaurant and head straight for Shantell's house. That would only lead to his associates clowning him some more. So he stayed and became the butt of their jokes, acting like everything was ok, although inside it was killing him.

Mike had to save face somehow. He knew that there was no way he was going to take this laying down. Pride was a dangerous thing. He wanted to pay back Shantell for her treason in the worst way.

Whether Shantell knew it or not, she was playing a dangerous game with a very dangerous man.

CHAPTER 14
MEET THE PARENTS

Shantell pulled her Sidekick out of her pocketbook to look at an incoming e-mail message. A bright smile quickly spread across her lips:

Long time no see? I really missed you! You missed me? LOL Can u meet my mom this evening? Can you join us for dinner? Are you available? Let me know. Give me a call later. And I'll e-mail you the directions to my house.

The e-mail was from Ronald. She had been expecting a call or something from him for some time now. When a few days went by with no word, Shantell began to worry. She thought maybe Ronald had changed his mind, that somehow he had lost interest. His e-mail helped to kill all her doubts. It erased all her worries and reaffirmed her faith in him.

She proceeded to punch in a few alphabetic keys to reply. As she did so, Shantell almost bumped into the other shoppers with her shopping cart in the Harris Teeter supermarket.

The truth of the matter was, Shantell didn't have anything to worry about. The reason why Ronald had taken so long was because he was trying to coordinate everyone's schedule, specifically his mother's, and he had a hectic schedule, too. the Bobcats had just returned from a four-game West Coast road trip. Now he was back and eager for Shantell and his mom to meet.

After re-reading the message for what seemed to be the hundredth time, Shantell flipped her Sidekick closed and re-entered the real world.

"Jordan, get over here," Shantell called out. "Leave that candy alone.

"Mommy, can I have this? Please! Please!" Jordan begged.

"Get it!" Shantell ordered. "And c'mon!"

She watched as her daughter bounced back up the aisle towards her. From that moment on, Shantell couldn't even think right. She went about her day, running errands, in a trance-like state. She was just going through the motions until she met up with Ronald and his mother.

๛

"Mommy, where we goin'?" Jordan questioned.

"I already told you already. We goin' to meet a friend of mine. Now Jordan, please be quiet. Mommy tryin' to concentrate. okay?" She gently replied.

Her daughter was a homebody. She was perfectly content with staying home and watching television. That was her idea of fun. Against her will, Shantell had to drag Jordan along to meet Ronald and his mother. They were a package deal; one couldn't have Shantell unless they accepted her daughter too. Tonight she would see if Ronald had any qualms about accepting this responsibility. Tonight she would see if Ronald and Jordan could get along.

Frustrated, young Jordan fell back in her seat and continued watching her favorite cartoon, Jimmy Neutron, on the portable DVD player.

Meanwhile, Shantell continued to drive, up interstate 77to Ronald's house in Lake Norm. As she did so, from time to time she glanced at her navigational system, to make sure she was going n the right way. Although, Lake Norm was a short distant outside of Charlotte's city limits, it might as well been out in the country for Shantell, because she had never been there.

Lake Norm was thought to be the home of the rich, similar to what the Hampton's were to New York City. A somewhat exclusive community that was surrounded by a large man-made lake, it was prime real estate in Charlotte for those who could afford the steep cost of owning a home there. For years there had been rumors floating around that rapper/entrepreneur Jay-Z had a huge mansion somewhere in Lake Norm.

Following her navigational system, Shantell turned onto the exit ramp. She followed its robotic instructions to a tee. The further Shantell drove, the darker it seemed to get. The area went from urban to almost rural and remote. As she drove down a dark, winding road, a deer darted out from the woods, causing her to slam on the brakes.

"Jordan, baby, are you alright?" She called out.

Jordan replied, "I'm okay."

"Goddamn! Stupid fuckin' deer!" Shantell cursed to herself.

From that point on, she drove more cautiously. She wasn't sure what would jump out of the woods next. Shantell felt it was better to be safe than sorry. She had some precious cargo onboard, her daughter; she couldn't afford to lose her.

Suddenly the house came into view. The lights from the house seemed to glow like eyes in the dark, and it was inviting. Pulling into the driveway, Shantell got a close-up view of the house. It was a beautiful Georgian style home.

Before Shantell could unfasten her seat belt, the front door swung open and out walked Ronald. Dressed casually in a white dress shirt and blue slacks, he strolled over to the car and opened the door.

"Did you have trouble finding my house?" he wondered.

"Let's just say, thank God for GPS," Shantell admitted. "You kinda way out here in the boondocks. Who you hidin' from?"

Ronald laughed the comment off. He proceeded to open the back door and unfasten Jordan from her car seat. Picking her up in his arms, he removed her from the car. Shantell was amazed that Jordan let Ronald continue to hold her. She was one of those kids who didn't take to strangers easily, and she hardly ever let anyone hold her except Shantell, so this was a good sign.

"This is your little girl you always talking about, huh? Jordan's her name, right?" he questioned. "She's so adorable. Jordan, one day you're going to make some guy a very lucky man."

After slamming the car doors shut, they walked towards the house. Shantell felt like she was walking the plank. Suddenly her stomach became unsettled; she had butterflies in her tummy. She was nervous about the meeting, to say the least.

"I'm glad you could make it," Ronald said. "But let me forewarn you, my mom can be a little bit of a snob, so don't take it personal. She's like that with everyone. And oh, by the way, I told her we met at the season opener. So go along with that, just in case she asks."

Now Shantell really wondered what she had gotten herself into. The picture Ronald had painted of his mother wasn't a nice one. Shantell decided to expect the worst but pray for the best.

When they walked in the house, Shantell realized that the inside was just as beautiful as the outside. She thought that a professional interior decorator helped furnish the house. Either that or his mother had excellent taste.

"Shantell would you like to see my place?" Ronald asked. "I'll take you on a brief tour."

"Sure, why not?"

Ronald proceeded to show her his five-bedroom, five-and-a-half bathroom, 4,000 square foot home that sat on two acres of land. By the time they finished taking a tour of his mini-mansion, which is how Ronald referred to it, Ronald's mother had magically appeared.

Dorothy Wright was seated in the living with her eyes glued to CNN, She was watching the President's State of the Union address.

"Mother, our guests are here," Ronald announced.

"Show them to the dining room," she commanded him. "I'll be there shortly."

She completely ignored her house guests and never once turned away from the television. Shantell thought that was so rude.

"Yes ma'am."

As they walked away Ronald turned and whispered to Shantell, "You'll have to excuse my mother, she really into politics. She always told me that foreign policy affects us here at home. She always has to know what's going on."

Ronald led Shantell and Jordan to the dining room, which was just a few feet away. The first thing that caught Shantell's eye was the lovely chandelier that hung high above the table yet lit up the room. Inside the dining room was a dining table big enough to seat Shantell's entire family. The mahogany wood table seemed to stretch the entire length of the room. The table was nicely decorated with a tablecloth, flower bouquets, candles, wine glasses, napkins and silverware.

The table had been set with painstaking care. Shantell almost didn't want to take a seat, out of fear that she or Jordan might mess something up. Reluctantly she did so anyway. She placed Jordan in a seat to her left and Ronald sat directly across from her. This left the head of the table open for his mother to sit whenever she arrived.

"Are you alright?" Ronald asked.

"I'm okay," she lied.

"You don't look so hot," he insisted.

"Don't be ridiculous. I'm fine. You seein' things," she assured him.

Though Shantell's mouth may have stated one thing, her body betrayed her. She looked tense. A smile hadn't passed her lips since she entered the house. Suddenly she was dead serious, and that wasn't her style.

"Jordan, put that spoon down before' I pop you!" she scolded her daughter. "Put it down now!"

As Jordan obeyed her mother, she suddenly burst out into tears. Shantell had her daughter trained to the tone of her voice. She didn't have to put her hands on Jordan; as soon she raised her voice, her daughter would shed tears.

Quickly Shantell came to the realization of what she had done. She began to comfort her daughter in an effort to keep her from making a scene; that she didn't need. Whatever she did worked because Jordan returned to her normal self in only a few moments.

At that very moment Dorothy Wright entered the room. She carried herself with great dignity, as if she were royalty. One look at her and it was easy to see where Ronald inherited his good looks.

"Good evening. You must be Shantell. And who might that be?"

"Who, her?" Shantell countered. "Oh, that's my daughter, Jordan."

"Oh really?" Dorothy said. "How old might that child be?"

"She's four and a half." Shantell answered. "She'll be five in November."

For some strange reason, Shantell didn't feel like Dorothy Wright's line of questioning was genuine. She felt like she was being interrogated and at some point in time, her answers might come back and haunt her. The thought made her uneasy. Shantell began to think about everything she said before she said it.

"How old were you when you had your child?" Dorothy questioned. "You had to be awfully young?"

Before Shantell could real give her a definitive answer or explanation to her question, Dorothy o popped yet another question. Sometimes Shantell was confused; she didn't know what answer to give to what question. She kept getting badgered by question after question, and Ronald was powerless to stop it.

"Do you believe in God?"
"What church do you go to?"
"Where are you from?"
"Where do you live?"
"Where did you attend school?"
"What was your major?"
"Where do you work?"
"What type of work do you do?"
"How did you meet my son?"

Now Shantell felt like she was filling out a job application, not dating Ronald. Dorothy really had an air of superiority about her, like she was better than everybody else and her son was too good for Shantell. She thought Ronald's mother was just nitpicking. Shantell didn't know that under any circumstances, Dorothy could be difficult to deal with. It was obvious to Shantell that Ronald's mother didn't care for her; this was made apparent by her attitude.

Shantell had been through a lot of bad experiences in her life, but she could never remember feeling this humiliated. She wanted to give Mrs. Wright a piece of her mind: curse her out, tell her off, let her know just who she was messing with. Out respect for her daughter, respect for Ronald and, more importantly respect for herself, she bit her tongue. Shantell refused to succumb to those devilish temptations. This was not the time to vent. She was going to conduct herself like a lady, even if it killed her.

The only time that Mrs. Wright stopped talking was during dinner. Even then, she managed to say a few choice words.

When the food was brought out, Shantell was really at a loss. She could barely pronounce these dishes, let alone eat them. The appetizer consisted of tequila shrimp and seared scallops on a bed of organic greens with dill tomatoes, corn and cucumbers. It got no better once the main course was served. They had lemon sorbet, peppercorn-crusted filet Mignon with brandy butter sauce. For dessert, they had chocolate decadence with lavender sabayon sauce.

Shantell didn't know how she managed to eat this bland meal. Probably trying to leave a good impression on Ronald had something to do with it. From time to time she glanced over at her daughter; this was one time she was happy that Jordan was playing with her food. Shantell made a mental note to herself to stop by the first McDonald's that they saw, on the way home.

The extended periods of silence at the table led Shantell to examine herself. She came to the instant realization that what she did didn't make her who she was. She had to do what she had to do. Granted, there were other options that she could have chosen, but she didn't, so she had to live with the consequences. Right or wrong, it was the cross she had to bear.

To her, life was a game of options. Some people just had more than others and on the other hand, some people did more with less.

When the dinner date was over, Mrs. Wright said a brief goodbye and excused herself from the table. Meanwhile, Ronald escorted Shantell and Jordan safely back to the car.

"Yo, I'm so proud of you," he stated. "You never cease to amaze me. You kept your cool in spite of all the mean things my mother said to you."

"Pppppsssss!" she sighed. "Only God knows how I managed to do dat. Yo' mother is really somethin' else. Where does she get off, talkin' to people like that? What, she perfect? Who she think she is, God's gift to the world? That woman needs to check herself."

"I know! I know!" Ronald insisted. "You're one hundred percent correct. But what can I do? I mean, should I disown her? A lot of people would love to have that problem. Some people don't have a mother."

The minute he said that, Ronald regretted his comments. He knew he messed up. Instantly he thought of Shantell's home situation and realized what a mistake he had just made.

"I'm sorry!" he apologized. "I wasn't directing that comment at you or anything."

"I know. Don't worry 'bout it. I didn't take it that way."

Ronald leaned inside the driver's door and gently pecked Shantell on the cheek. The kiss did wonders for her spirit. After all she had been through she needed a little pick-me up.

This tender moment was interrupted by Mrs. Wright.

"Ronald, it's a little chilly out there. Do you think you should come out of that air before you catch a cold, or the flu?" she called out.

"Alright, Mother. I'll be right there,." he yelled. "Coming!"

Ronald turned just in time to see his mother retreat back inside the house. He sighed aloud once she was out of earshot. Even her act was wearing thin with him.

"Get home safely," he told Shantell. "Be careful on your way back home; there are lots of deer running through these woods this time of night. Text me as soon as you get home, so I'll know you made it home safely."

Shantell placed the key inside the ignition and cranked her car up. In seconds she disappeared back down the long, spiraling road. She thought to herself that this was it. Her relationship with Ronald was over. Surely his mother was going to poison her against him; she would bet her life on it.

'Hey, that's his loss.' She thought. 'And the next man's gain. Oh, well!'

In her rearview mirror she took one last look at Ronald's house. Shantell was almost certain that she would never see it again.

CHAPTER 15

IT'S A SMALL WORLD

Entering the Bobcat Arena, Shantell looked up into the sky and smiled. Seemingly she was thanking her lucky stars. She was feeling much better these days. It was Dorothy Wright who was the one that was hurting. Over the past few weeks the two women had engaged in a tug-of-war over Ronald. Ultimately, it was Shantell who emerged victorious.

Shantell and Ronald were now an item despite all the nonsense his mother had fed him about Shantell. For once in his life, he stood up to his mother and went against her wishes. Ronald had chosen Shantell and he had caught hell for it. It wasn't easy for Ronald to defy his mother, especially for the first time. Somehow, he summoned enough courage to do so.

Now Shantell could laugh while remembering some of the late-night calls she had received from Ronald. Somehow she found all the negative comments about her so funny now. "She's a gold digger! All she wants is your money. How could you settle for a hoochie like her? I brought you up better than that. You make me ashamed to say you're my son," Dorothy Wright would say.

In the midst of all this confusion, Shantell was his Rock of Gibraltar, unwavering in her support. Shantell was the one who helped Ronald through this tough period in his life. She taught Ronald how to man up. She showed him how to express himself to his mother without being disrespectful. She made him realize it was okay to agree to disagree. She made him see that this may have been their first disagreement but surely it wouldn't be their last. Ronald was like a bird Shantell was teaching to spread his wings and fly the coop.

In turn, he appreciated everything she did for him. Ronald began showing his appreciation in the form of lavish gifts, shopping sprees and weekend getaways. One day, out of the blue, he gave Shantell a four-carat, diamond friendship ring. His true gratitude went way beyond anything of significance that he could purchase for her. Ronald was thankful that Shantell had come into his life when she had. She was a welcomed addition.

Despite her newfound celebrity and her status as Ronald's girlfriend, Shantell didn't act entitled. She didn't change because she was in now. She didn't suddenly become greedy. She took whatever Ronald gave her and never asked for anything. This kind of behavior made Ronald feel that she was there for him and not for the lifestyle he could provide, as his mother had once claimed.

"Ticket, ma'am," an usher called out.

"Wait a minute, please!" she replied. "I gotta find it."

Reaching into her clutch bag, Shantell produced her ticket. The usher scanned it and Shantell was allowed admittance into the arena. Ronald had provided her with season tickets, courtside seats, whenever the team was in town. She was front row and center, cheering them on.

All of a sudden it seemed like the Charlotte Bobcat's game was the hottest ticket in town. The team had gotten off to a good start, winning seven out of its first ten games. Around town there was even talk of making the playoffs. Finally, the team was being taken seriously by the league and the fans. It was no longer a laughingstock expansion team. The Bobcats were no longer pushovers. They weren't an easy win on someone's schedule any more. The perception of the team had undergone a drastic overhaul; they went from pretenders to contenders. Every night rabid fans packed the arena. The arena was sold out for every game.

All of the hoopla that had engulfed the city was partly due to Ronald Wright. His play was part of the reason the

Bobcats were off to such a good start. The rookie had taken the league by storm. He had served notice to the veterans that he was a force to be reckoned with. Though Ronald may have been a rookie, he played like anything but. He alone was worth the cost of admission.

Sitting down in her courtside seat, Shantell watched the pre-game festivities. About a dozen or so cheerleaders went through a high-energy dance routine. When they were finished, the two teams came onto the court for the pre-game shoot around. Tonight's opponents were the New York Knicks. Several times Ronald and Shantell made eye contact. After the warm ups, Ronald had a habit of totally ignoring her. He didn't allow anything to distract him from the game.

When it came to playing basketball, Ronald was superstitious. Before arriving at the arena he liked to have a pre-game meal of homemade hamburgers and French fries. He washed that down with a Coke. At his locker, while he dressed for the game, he liked to listen to some rap music on his iPod, usually some tunes by Kanye West. Music relaxed him, but at the same time it got his focused. He never deviated from this routine.

"Would everyone please stand for the national anthem?" the announcer solemnly asked.

A local gospel artist took center court and sung a soulful rendition of the national anthem. The game was almost set to begin.

"Ladies and gentlemen make some noise for your Charlotte Bobcats!" the announcer yelled.

The enthusiastic crowd roared for the home team. The team was given a standing ovation. There was electricity in the air; truly this had the making of special season.

"Starting at shooting guard from Duke University, number twenty-three, Ronald Wright!"

Shantell was ecstatic; she had no idea that Ronald was going to be inserted into tonight's starting lineup. She clapped long and extra hard for him. Shantell was behind him 110 %.

From the tip-off, the game was like a track meet. Ronald made his presence felt. He scored eight points in the first three minutes, using a variety of ways. He scored on dunks, jump shots and free throws. He took whatever scoring opportunities the defense gave him.

Meanwhile, Shantell would be seen and heard cheering him on wildly. During the second quarter, Ronald was fouled particularly hard by the opposing team, but there was no foul called. Shantell was livid. As he laid there on the floor momentarily shaken up. Shantell got up out of her seat and began to give the referee an earful.

"Hey, ref, where's the fuckin' foul!" she shouted. "Stevie Wonder could have seen that! I thought this was basketball, not football!"

The cameraman's timing couldn't have been better. He captured Shantell as she ripped into the referee for the blown foul call. Instantly her image flashed across every screen in the arena. The crowd applauded her efforts.

Out of the tens of thousands of people in attendance, there was one person didn't find her so entertaining. That person was Mike. He was seething in his seat. The sight of Shantell made him mad all over again.

Time and time again, he had reached out to Shantell by leaving messages on her home and cellular phones. He even dropped by her house a few times. Whatever he tried, it didn't seem to work. Either Shantell didn't return his calls or she wasn't around to see him. No matter what way Mike chose to look at it, he felt neglected and ignored. He was about to put an end to that feeling right now.

"Yo, wait right here. I'll be right back," he explained. "I'm goin' to go say hi to a friend."

"Alright," his friend replied. "Could you bring me back some chips and something to drink?"

"A'ight!" Mike walked down the stairs and marched directly toward Shantell. She was too involved in the game to even see him coming.

"Pssss! Pssss! Excuse me, miss."

Shantell turned in response to the catcall. When she saw Mike, her heart dropped. To her, it wasn't the time or place to be seen with Mike. What if Ronald saw them together? What would he think? At this point, Shantell's guilty conscience was getting the better of her.

"Damn, you all dat now?" Mike said aloud. "You can't even return a nigger's calls no more? Wow!"

Shantell didn't like the undertone of his conversation. Mike's presence alone made her feel uneasy. Still, there was nothing she could say in her defense, so Shantell remained silent.

He continued, "Yo, take a walk wit' me to the concession stand. Lemmie holla at ya for minute."

Before leaving her seat, Shantell nervously looked over at the Bobcat's bench to see what Ronald was doing. He was being attended to by the personal trainer, who blocked his view.

Quickly, Shantell followed Mike and they headed up the stairs to the concession stand. As soon as they reach the corridor, Mike stopped dead in his tracks.

"What the fuck is up wit' you? You really tryin' to play a nigger, huh? You got wit' this nigger and you actin' all brand new," Mike spat. "Bitch, don't forget I made you. I copped you that whip, I put you up in that crib. This is how you pay me back? You know what? You an ungrateful ass- hoe. I shoulda left yo' ass right where I found you! "

Through all his hooting and hollering, Mike had to admit that Shantell looked better than ever. He couldn't take his eye off her. How he wished for old times again.

Normally Shantell would have met his aggression with some of her own. She would have cursed Mike out. But this wasn't the same girl from the hood. Truth be told, this was what .Mike was expecting. He wanted to make a scene in public. Shantell didn't even feed into his rhetoric. She thought it went deeper than that. His mouth was saying one thing and his body yet another. Still, she let him get it off his chest. When he was finished she spoke.

"Look, I don't see what you're so mad at?" Shantell stated. "You got somebody, don't you? You go home to yo' girlfriend every night, so how can you be mad at anything I do? You do your thing, why can't I do mine?"

Secretly, Shantell suspected it wasn't an issue of what she was doing. Rather, it was who she was doing it with. Ronald was a serious upgrade over Mike. And Mike knew it, too. The fact that Shantell was doing good without him was a hurting feeling. To her, Mike had to deal with it. Mike was the one who laid down the ground rules in the first place. It was supposed to be a just-be-good-to-me type of relationship. A see-you-when-I-see-you thing.

Mike totally ignored everything Shantell had to say, despite how right she may have been. Her words went in one ear and out the other. They had no effect on his temperament. He was furious.

"Bitch, if we weren't here, at the arena, I swear I'd knock you the fuck out!"

"What? Listen to you. You know how you sound?" Shantell stated.

"Ho, I don't give a fuck how I sound!" he barked. "Say one more word and I will slap the shit out of you."

At this point Shantell began to cautiously back away from Mike. She was trying to get out of arms reach just in case he made good on his threat.

"Look, I don't know why you even taken' it there. But since you feel like that, do me a favor and come get that shit up outta my house. That way, you ain't never gotta deal wit' me ever in life."

"I will be over there when I get there. You leave that shit right where it's at!" Mike said.

Shantell warned, "Look, I'm not askin' you, I'm tellin' you. Come get yo' shit. It ain't like that no more!"

"You heard what I said!" Mike growled.

"No, you heard what I said. Don't have me call the muthafuckin' cops. Come get yo' shit."

Threatening Mike with the police definitely caught his attention. He didn't play those types of games. If looks could kill, Shantell would be dead right now.

Instantly she realized the mistake she had made. Still, she couldn't retract her words. What was said couldn't be unsaid. Shantell was merely trying to express to Mike how badly she wanted the drugs out of her house and how badly she wanted him out of her life. Too bad she picked the wrong choice of words. Now she had to live with the consequences.

Quickly Mike came to his senses and he backed off Shantell. His tough guy stance disappeared because he didn't want any problems with the law.

"Aright! You got that. I'll be over after the game." He announced.

Immediately after that they went there separate ways. Shantell went back to her seat to enjoy the rest of the game. Meanwhile, Mike returned to his seat to stew in his own anger.

Shantell wasn't a fool; she had to know that Mike wouldn't tolerate her threat. She felt threatened by him; she didn't know exactly what he would do. Still, Shantell felt he would do something. She just didn't know what. She knew something was coming; the question was, could she handle it?

❧❦❧

Shantell arrived home later that night after waiting for Ronald to shower and dress. She decided to leave Jordan at the babysitter's. She would pick her up early the next morning. Cautiously she entered her complex; Shantell was still mindful of the spat she had with Mike earlier that day. She sat in her car a few minutes, carefully surveying the landscape, when she was sure the cost was clear. Shantell exited the car and entered the house. When Shantell flicked on the lights, she couldn't believe what she saw.

Her house was wrecked. It looked like a tornado had swept through there. Everything of value was broken or destroyed. Her big screen television had a hole kicked in it. Food was thrown all over the kitchen. Her daughter's room was even vandalized. All of Shantell's clothes, as well as Jordan's, were stolen or destroyed.

Shantell broke down, falling to the floor in the middle of the wreckage and cried her eyes out. Not so much for herself, but for Jordan. There were irreplaceable personal items that were damaged, stolen or destroyed.

There was no doubt in Shantell's mind who was behind this: Mike. If he didn't personally do it, then he had a hand in it somehow. Shantell had carefully inspected the house for signs of forced entry. She saw none. The only person who had access to her apartment was Mike. Beside her, he was the only other person with a key.

With no family to turn to for help, Shantell reached out to the only person she could, Ronald. She pulled out her cell phone and dialed his number.

"Hello, Ronald." She sobbed. "Somebody just broke into my house and fucked up my place. All my shit is either stolen or ruined. They even messed up my daughter's things. I don't know what I'm gonna do."

"Shantell, listen to me. Calm down. I can barely understand you," Ronald said. "Now, run that by me again."

Taking a deep breath, Shantell slowly repeated what she had just said. This time it was audible and understandable to Ronald.

"Did you call the police?" he asked.

"No. I am still kinda messed up about the whole situation. I was tryin' to take a tally of what was taken to see what was damaged and what can I still salvage."

"Listen, I'm on my way over there right now," Ronald announced. "Everything is going to be alright."

No truer words were ever spoken.

The very next day, Ronald placed a series of calls to his agent and his financial adviser. Before the day was over, he had secured Shantell a luxurious condominium in The Arlington, in the south end section of Charlotte known as Dilworth.

Ronald was the answer to all Shantell's problems. He waved his magical wand, money, over the situation and Shantell's troubles just disappeared. When Ronald was done working his magic, Shantell's home situation was better than before.

Mike may have thought he was hurting her, but actually he had helped her.

CHAPTER 16
HAPPILY EVER AFTER

It was late Sunday afternoon when Mike finally awoke from his long slumber. He had been sleeping off the effects of wild partying, heavy drinking and a hot sexual romp. He moved slowly through the house, still feeling the aftermath of all three things. His energy level was nowhere near it should be. Mike was cool with that; he knew that this wasn't anything a long nap couldn't cure.

After brushing his teeth, the first thing on his mind was reading the Sunday paper. Mike was a sports fanatic; he needed to know what went on in the world of sports while he was asleep. If he missed a day of either watching ESPN's *Sports Center* or reading the daily paper, he felt that his day didn't go right. He couldn't function not being in the know.

"Yo, where's the paper?" he asked.

Tonya sat in the living room, watching TV, totally ignoring Mike. As usual, his girlfriend was mad at him again. This was because of Mike's tardiness; he kept late hours in the street. Tonya suspected that he was cheating on her but she couldn't prove it. She had warned him time and time again, "Don't let the sun beat you home." Mike had violated her rule so many times, it was pathetic.

He repeated, "Yo, where's the fuckin' paper? Stop actin' stupid! You too old for that."

"Why don't you look for it?" Tonya snapped. "It's sittin' right there, on the fuckin' kitchen table. If it was a snake, it woulda bit yo' ass. You kill me wit' that, Mike. You don't never look for nothin'.''

"Who you talkin' to like that? Yo, watch yo' fuckin' mouth! .Don't let yo' mouth write a check yo' ass can't cash," Mike barked.

"Whateva nigga!" Tonya countered.

"Okay, keep it up. I ain't gonna tell you no more. Think I'm playin' if you wanna."

With that said, Mike marched through living room, toward the kitchen, in search of the Sunday paper. There he found a fresh copy of the *Charlotte Observer* newspaper lying neatly on the table. He pulled out his chair and casually began going through the paper. Mike went directly to the sports page. The caption read, "Rookie Leads the Way in Triple Overtime Win". Accompanying the large article was a black-and-white picture of Ronald catching an alley-oop dunk.

"Bitch-ass nigger!" he cursed.

"What?" Tonya replied.

"Mind yo' business. Wasn't nobody even talkin' to you!" He shouted.

Quickly Mike discarded the sports section on the floor. He didn't want to see or read about Ronald Wright's exploits on the basketball court. He wasn't the least bit impressed by him. In Mike's book, Ronald would never be the half the man he was. He was self-made. A sport didn't define him. He felt if you took away the millions of dollars that Ronald earned on and off the court, he was nobody.

Mike tried to put Ronald out his mind by glancing through other sections of the paper. He scanned the front page and the local section but found nothing of interest. He moved right along to the entertainment section and finally, to the life section of the paper. There he read the horoscopes and the advice column. Flipping through that section he came to the part where couples announced their engagement. Mike looked on in interest to see if he could spot any of his bitches.

He saw a bunch of white couples and a few mixed couples. Just he was about to turn the page, something caught his eye. If seeing is believing, than Mike refused to believe what he saw. There was a picture of Shantell and Ronald, announcing their engagement.

Would you look at this shit here? He mused.

For months Mike had heard all the talk around town, about Shantell and Ronald, how they were supposed to be getting married, and he had had it up to here with it. Now it was staring him right in the face.

Words could not describe just how Mike felt at this moment. As he read on, his blood began to boil. The finality of the situation was beginning to set in. In Mike's warped and twisted mind, Shantell belonged to him. He made her. Matter of fact, he saved her from the uncertain future of a stripper.

Quietly, Mike still held out for some sort of reconciliation. He was ready to admit he messed up, and he was about to apologize for all that he done, if only Shantell would take him back. He felt like the acts he had committed against her were forgivable. They were like crimes of passion, because he wasn't in his right state of mind.

So much for that, he thought.

As he continued to stare at the picture, he noticed that the couple looked happy. Shantell looked happier than he had ever seen her, and that infuriated Mike. He was miserable in his current situation and he wanted her to be miserable too.

Mike had done everything in his power to get back at Shantell, including burglarizing her apartment and stealing her car. But it seemed like none of his shenanigans worked. Somehow, they had backfired on him. Every time he destroyed something of value that he had bought, Ronald merely upgraded the item to something much better. The things he did seemed to draw them closer together.

Regardless of the fact that Mike wasn't with Shantell any more, or hadn't had her sexually in months, she still was his. Mike felt that he was the one that gave Shantell her first taste of the finer things in life. Now this ungrateful bitch was running off and getting married on him. There was no way Mike could allow that. He vowed that they would get married over his dead body.

∙∙∙

It was a picturesque day in Charlotte, North Carolina. There wasn't a cloud in the sky and the sun shone brightly on the city. Originally, the forecast had called for scattered showers but there wasn't a cloud in the sky. God must have showed Shantell favor on her wedding day. Thus far, He chose not to spoil it. Shantell prayed that the weather would hold, at least for the sake of her wedding pictures.

Shantell opted not to push for an extravagant wedding on some remote tropical island, the kind of wedding that every woman dreams of. Though she probably could have;, she had Ronald wrapped around her finger. He would do anything to make her happy. All she had to do was say the word. Since his mother was not only coordinating the wedding but controlling the purse strings, she decided to live with whatever she got. Whatever Dorothy Wright decided was okay with her.

Every day, for the rest of her life or as long as she was married to Ronald, Shantell knew she had to prove herself to his mother. She had to prove she wasn't the gold digger that his mother claimed she was, first by signing a prenuptial agreement and secondly, by accepting a modest wedding ceremony.

Ronald's mother felt and would always feel like he son was making a big mistake. She felt that Shantell wasn't worthy of her son. But after countless talks with Ronald, her husband and their pastor, she relented. She agreed to let her son live his life and make his own mistakes. She was there to ensure it wouldn't be a financial one.

For her wedding there was one expensive purchase Shantell was allowed to make, and that was for a designer wedding dress. She wore a $20,000 wedding dress by Vera

Wang. The stylish dress looked stunning on Shantell. Her body breathed life into it.

Ronald stood proudly as he watched Shantell walk slowly towards him. He smiled lovingly at his soon-to-be stepdaughter Jordan, as she threw down a trail of rose petals. He considered himself a lucky man, despite what anyone else had thought. He knew that some of his teammates didn't approve of his marriage to Shantell, because most of them knew her background as a stripper. Still, it didn't matter to him what they thought about him. He didn't care what they had to say about the situation, either. He had already discussed this with his pastor and he told him. "Son, they talked about Jesus too."

When Shantell walked through the church doors, all eyes had been on her. She now strolled gracefully down the aisle toward her future husband. The whereabouts of her father were unknown, so she got an older distant male cousin to give her way.

Damn, you beautiful! Ronald thought to himself. *Thank you, Lord, for sending this blessing my way.*

As Shantell got closer to the wedding party she tried not to focus on Ronald at all. Just looking at him might make her cry. Instead, she began to concentrate on her daughter. This was a momentous occasion for her too.

She was about to give Jordan the father figure she never had. Shantell was about to give her daughter's life some stability. The irony of the entire situation was that young Jordan would never know about the life her mother led or the things she had to do to feed her. For that, Shantell was eternally grateful.

Their new life would bare a stark contrast to her old one. A change had finally come.

This was a bittersweet day for Shantell. She was upset that her mother couldn't be here to share in her day. Ronald's family members outnumbered hers by at least twenty to one.

Finally the moment had arrived. The couple stood face to face, lost in each other's eyes. After the pastor recited the formalities, Shantell and Ronald recited their own wedding vows, just like they had planned.

Ronald began, "I love you, Shantell. Today is a very special day. Long ago, you were just a dream and a prayer. This day is like a dream come true, because the Lord himself answered my prayer. For today, Shantell, you as my joy have become my crown. I thank Jesus for the honor and opportunity of journeying through life with you. Thank you for being what you are to me. With our futures as bright as the promise of God, I will care for you, honor, respect and protect you. I will lay down my life for you, Shantell, my friend, my love. Today, I give you me."

Shantell softly said, "I love you, Ronald Wright, with all my heart and soul. And you know this to be true. For years I prayed that God would lead me to His choice and I am confident that His will is being fulfilled today. Christ told us that the wife must submit herself unto her own husband as unto the Lord. For as Christ is the Head of His Church, so is the husband head of his wife. Ronald, I submit myself to you."

Everyone was moved by there vows. There wasn't a dry eye in the church. People looked on in envy as Ronald and Shantell marched down the aisle as Mr. and Mrs. Ronald Wright.

From her seat, Dorothy Wright stewed. Outwardly her smiling face gave off the impression of happiness, but it was all an act. She couldn't wait for Shantell to slip up, so she could get into Ronald's ear and have him file for divorce. She wanted Shantell to go back to the ghetto existence from which she came.

There were no immediate plans for a honeymoon. The NBA season was still underway. Ronald's job took full precedence over everything else. Shantell didn't care about traveling, anyway. She had survived all her life without leaving Charlotte; she didn't feel like she was missing anything.

As the couple strolled out the church, they were greeted by hundreds of fans and spectators who had gathered outside to get a glimpse of this celebrity wedding. They smiled and waved at the swarm of people, as they proceeded toward their limousine.

Suddenly out of the corner of his eye, Ronald could see a shadowy figure rapidly approaching. He noticed a large black object in the figure's right hand. Ronald's heart was racing with fear. Ever alert, at the last possible minute he shoved his bride to the floor of the limo.

The loud crackle of gunfire shattered the tranquility of the afternoon. Calmly, the assailant managed to squeeze off two shots before he was subdued by a group of innocent bystanders.

The crowd looked on in horror, unsure of what they had just witnessed. In slow motion, Ronald seemed to fall to the ground as Shantell let out a blood-curdling scream. A sickening feeling hit her.

"Nnnnnnnooooooooo!!!!!" She shouted. "Nnnnoooo!!"

Fearing for her daughter's life, Shantell began a frantic search in the crowd for Jordan with her eyes. Quickly she spotted her, crouching low, with a groomsman shielding her. Shantell crawled over to her dead husband's lifeless body. She pounded on his chest and pleaded for him to wake. Soon blood drenched her beautiful wedding dress; Shantell couldn't believe what had happened.

Her fairy tale wedding had turned into a tragic nightmare right before her very eyes.

EPILOGUE

No one at that wedding would ever forget that fateful day. News of the tragedy spread like wildfire. Ronald Wright's murder made national headlines. Old wounds were re-opened for the city of Charlotte and its residents. Once again, their judicial system was examined by the world with a microscope. The city was forced to endure another high-profile trial involving an elite athlete.

Subsequently, Mike Boogie was tried and convicted, by a jury of his peers, for the murder of Ronald Wright. He received two life sentences. Never would he walk the streets of Charlotte again. Though Mike may have pulled the trigger, what really killed Ronald were hatred, jealousy and envy.

Shantell Bryant, widow of the deceased, became embroiled in a lengthy legal dispute of her late husband's estate. Being that she lacked the proper funds to secure adequate legal services, her claims were dismissed in civil court.

During the trial Shantell and Mike's former relationship had been exposed. This led Dorothy Wright to blame Shantell for her son's death indirectly. Dorothy felt that Shantell was responsible because she never made Ronald aware of the situation between her and Mike. This was an unforgivable act, more than the minor oversight that the prosecutor claimed. Dorothy had even filed a civil lawsuit of her own, a wrongful death suit, naming Shantell as the defendant.

Shantell was legally put out of her condominium. Everything that Ronald bought her, his mother took back. Shantell wound up pawning the engagement and wedding rings he gave her just to make it. For a time, Shantell and Jordan would sleep in a homeless shelter. That was, until she started stripping again. Rumor has it that she's right back in the hood where she started.

As for Ronald Wright, who knows? He might have been one of the NBA's all-time greats with all that natural talent he possessed. He might have been mentioned in the same breathe as Michael Jordan, Magic Johnson and Larry Bird, or even the Lebron James's, Carmelo Anthony's or Dwayne Wades of today. He might have gone down in NBA history, leaving a legacy, had it not been for fate's cruel intervention.

An Afterthought

In a perfect world, young Black females like Shantell Bryant wouldn't exist. But unfortunately, we don't live in a perfect world, so they do. They are alive and well in every major urban city across the United States, young girls willing to do any and everything to get ahead.

To truly be able to assess the problem, we have to delve into these kid's backgrounds. What are their social and economical statuses? Who are their parents? Who are these children being raised by? Under what conditions? Nowadays, babies are literally raising babies. The same sacrifices that older generation's parents made are not being made for them. It's sad but true.

I'd like to say, in parting, to all the young girls, women and sisters: life is a game of options. Some of us have more options than others. Even when you think you don't have any, you have a few. Remember the wrong way will always be there. So give the right way a chance first. The street life ain't everything that they say it is.

Other Titles
by Dynasty Publishing

Little Ghetto Girl
by Danielle Santiago

Swingers
by Torrian Ferguson

Cha-Ching
by Tonya Blount

Country Boy
by Alan Little

Ana's Magic
by Adia Mckenzie

To order visit
www.dynastybooks.com

ATTENTION WRITERS!

Dynasty Publishing is currently seeking new authors of urban fiction including poetry, testimonies and autobiographies.

Submission Guidelines

- Synopsis and first four chapters required
- Typed, double-space, 1 ½ inch margins all around and only on one side of the page
- 12-point font in Times New Roman
- Cover letter stating address, phone number, the type of work being submitted
- A photo of author

No manuscripts will be returned. Please include a self-addressed, stamped envelope for a prompt response.

All manuscripts should be addressed to:

Dynasty Publishing
Attn: Submissions
5585 Central Avenue
Charlotte, NC 28212

Check us out on the web for information on our latest publications and featured authors at www.dynastybooks.com